RAYNE

LUMINESCENCE

Book One of the RAYNE Trilogy

QUOLEENA SBROCCA

To my boys,
Angelo, Nico, & Phoenix
&
For my niece,
Rayne

CONTENTS

LUMINESCENCE (n): possessing the ability to transform invisible forms of energy into visible light

BIOLUMINESCENCE (n): production and emission of light by a living organism

Prelude

By the late 22nd century, all natural resources were depleted.
The largest of beasts which once roamed the Earth and swam the oceans
became extinct. Generations of warfare destroyed civilization. The
planet was at its pinnacle of suffering.

…But nature always finds a way to thrive, and this time Earth's most
intelligent species has evolved.

Now threats to the environment are extinguished. Harmony prevails.
The Earth is restored to its youth.

At the dawn of The Rebirth Period, a new species of humans dominates
the Earth. Possessing the ability to understand all dialects, they estab-
lish a universal language and call it The Standard.

In the first hours of their second year of life, *Homo praestans* experience
the Luminescence and awaken to a mystical ability.

Except one. Her name is Rayne.

This is her story.

1

Dawn stirs me, and I awake with a peculiar feeling. I don't know why I feel nauseous. I roll to my stomach, hoping it will help. I close my eyes and wince as the memory of what happened flood my senses.

I know at precisely 2 a.m. I awoke with the sensation that my chamber was spinning, and my body was hurtling through space. My garments were soaked with my sweat, and coldness consumed me. In the darkness I stumbled to my chamber wash room, the contents of my stomach threatening to spill to the floor. I don't remember how long I remained crouched beside my latrine, my back pressed against the cool, glossy wall. I also don't remember returning to my sleep pod. I do know I had the strangest dreams.

Now it is morn. I'm exhausted, and I have an odd feeling something is different. I feel it in my bones. Cold. Tingling.

I've heard others describe this, and it confuses me. If this is the same thing, it's 15 years late.

I shake my head at the thought. It's impossible. I'm simply—and randomly—ill. I try to ignore the lingering dizziness. I nestle deeper in my pod and focus on its cradling comfort. My arms stretch above my head, and I brush the soft, shimmering fabric secured to two Great Oaks at either end.

I roll to my side and focus on the thick trunk at my feet, its roots burrowing into the ground below my chamber. The tree contrasts the surface of my floor. It's an aggregate of rusted metals and clear and black plastics, smooth to the touch and always soothingly warm.

I blink a few times and rub my face to shake off the last bits of sleepy haze. My eyes trace the floor and linger on the walls. I imagine what the plaster and brick feel like below the glossy, protective coating. I think of when I was at Primary, and we discussed the history of Homo sapiens—the Ancients. They're all extinct now. We have preserved what foundations survived their wars with protective layers, so as not to waste materials.

As my mind drifts, I welcome it. It often does in these first moments of waking. I would rather ponder ancient history than experience the world outside my chamber walls. But I can't stay in here indefinitely.

It is *dies Gandhi*—the day of Gandhi—what the Ancients in this realm called Sunday. It's the day we return to Institute after three days off. Everyone pretty much ignores me, except a certain band of comrades. They've taunted me since Primary. They do it because I'm different.

They say I'm more like the Homo sapiens than our species. In truth, I'm like my peers in every way except which matters most: the Luminescence. It's the most significant, innate distinction between us and them.

To everyone else, it brings one of ten abilities. All are crucial to society and to this Earth. I possess no ability. Therefore, I'm still Unregistered, like an infant. I have nothing to contribute to my colony.

As the dizziness lingers, I fantasize this has changed. I know it's impossible. The Luminescence only comes the night of the second year of birth. It never did for me.

I remember waking that morn to see my mater's and pater's weary faces. They slept in my room that night to await the course of nausea, vomiting, and cold sweats which never came. It brought me to tears. It was the first time my pater regarded me with disappointment. It was the day my mater stopped knowing how to relate to me.

I think of it, and my face flushes. It's not due to the heartbreak I felt. It's because of something I nearly forgot. This is the day of my birth. It's my seventeenth year, and in four weeks, I will be of age. I will be free from my obligations of Institute, and I can leave this colony for good if I wish.

My heart soars when I remember something else. None are expected to uphold their duties on such a day. I stretch and grin and release a quiet squeal in delight.

I was born on a *dies Hypatia*, in Decumensis—the tenth month. Hypatia was a mathematician, philosopher, and astronomer. She was also one of the early Homo praestans. As I lie in my pod, I recite a few names of others. Gandhi. da Vinci. Confucius. Tolstoy. Bach. Aristotle. All their histories and secret journals are preserved on the cyber database. Hundreds of them lived during the age when the planet was dominated by the Ancients. I gaze at nothing in particular and wonder what it must have been like for them to hide the truth of their existence and their abilities.

I hear the soft steps of my mater outside my chamber. It's her way of gently urging me to join her for morning sustenance. I unwrap myself from my pod's caressing material and lower my feet to the warm floor. I dangle my legs over the edge and study the muscles of my deep-tan calves.

From the moment we can speak, we learn the physical differences between us and the Ancients. Our arms hang a few centimeters longer; our calf muscles are bulkier; our chests are narrower, because our lungs are more efficient. The air in The Rebirth Period is pure. Pollution is a word we only know in theory.

I hear her footsteps again. It's time to confront the day. I force myself to stand. The thin material of my garment clings to me. If it was proper for my mater to enter my chamber now, she would see visual evidence of my turbulent night.

I enter my wash room and use the glossy surface of the wall to see my reflection. I release my hair from its bun. Wavy locks of my scarlet-brown hair fall into my face and tickle the tip of my keen nose. It's always a task to style my hair in a presentable state. I usually allow it to hang wild and free.

My mater urges me to cut it short. Since it's wavy and requires more effort to maintain, it would be a display of etiquette to do so. I refuse. My age peers say it's my genetic defect which drives me to defy social norms of proper grooming. I ignore their trivial comments. I've always been an outlander in my colony. I may as well look the part.

I apply my paint in the usual manner. My method is the same each day, though I vary the colors based on my mood. The glossy wall offers a meager reflection, but it's enough. It's the only time I really see my features. My face is narrow with prominent cheeks. The lids of my eyes are wide, and the ridge of my brow is defined. My nose is long, and my mouth is small.

On the morn of my thirteenth year, my mater watched my first attempt, coaching me on how best to highlight my facial features. I could only see hints of my effort, but I considered it a success. I remember her saying the result was "not suitable to social expectations." She made me wash it off so she could do it properly.

I bind my hair in secure ties so it hangs to my back in a tidy bunch. It's the way I style it when guests come to our domus for an evening of sustenance and socialization. I do it now to appease my mater, since it's my day of birth.

Before I leave my chamber, I dress myself for the seasonal temperature. Though we each maintain our own sense of style, the amount of fabric is the same: minimal to refrain from excess and waste.

I select a top piece the color of the midday sky. It tapers below my rib cage, and its sleeves cover the full length of my arms. I dress in black bottoms which rest low on my waist and cover my upper legs. The material below my knees hangs in stiff flaps which extend to my ankles. The lustrous material is a blend of textile fabric and buffalo hide. I select a deep-blue pair of foot soles from my chamber wardrobe and step onto them. The material seals to my skin.

The last thing I do is slip my holodigit onto my left thumb and index finger. A glass casing, sealing two small discs, covers my fingertips. A thin layer of silicone conceals the glass. It covers the full length of my fingers, like an extra layer of skin. It's an information database and an activity and communication device. I'm never without it.

My cleansing has revived me, and the dizziness seems to be waning. I wave my hand over a small, silver panel on the wall. My chamber barrier deactivates, and I enter the corridor. The glossy coating enhances the pale-gray walls, for a soothing ambience.

The floor throughout the main quarters is composed of petrified moss and bark. It's lustrous and soothing to the senses. I navigate the Aspen trees which line the corridor. Like the Great Oaks in my chamber, their roots lie deep beneath the floor of our villa, and their trunks extend through the roof.

I reach the culina and see my mater washing containers and vessels. She offers a slight nod and polite wink in greeting. I see the profile of my pater and the glow of his holofield communication. He sits on our metallic and concrete bench in the corner of the room. It's his usual place for conducting his affairs of the morn. He is a sciens, and his duty is to design and maintain our technological infrastructure.

I know my parentes will not offer to spend this day with me. They have not done so since the morn of my second year. When I was an infant, they adopted me with no knowledge of my genetic deficiency. I believe they would not have done so had they known.

It was never a mystery their blood does not flow through my veins. I look nothing like either of them. I wish I did. Perhaps then they could have ignored my defect if they truly felt I was their own.

Both of them have silky hair the color of raven. Unlike

mine, theirs behaves with the slightest brush of their fingers. Their skin is an olive, pale-tan; mine is deep tan. Our eyes are the same dark brown, but that's where the similarity ends.

Their interaction with me is always laden with polite obligation. It's been a few revolutions of the sun since I hoped for more.

When I enter the culina, my pater turns to greet me in his usual manner of terse politeness. He prefers his associates neither see nor hear me. He claims it reduces the instances of their passive-aggressive remarks.

My mater also does not speak. She gestures for me to remain silent—as if I need the reminder. It's been the same each morn for 15 years.

She leads me outside to our veranda. The air is still crisp at this hour. When I step onto the smooth slats of recycled wood, I see my mater has already prepared my favorite morning fare: pomegranate juice, four quail eggs topped with fresh kale and arugula, and a few pieces of peppered shrimp. I offer a genuine smile at this annual maternal act.

"Good day of birth to you, dear Rayne. May you find your seventeenth year to be ripe with intellectual and emotional abundance." It's her annual greeting.

"A universe of appreciation to you, Mater. May I bring joy to you and Pater in this my final month with you."

I try to suppress the excitement as I speak the words, but I think she notices the twinkle in my eyes. In one month, I'll be free from my status as a subordinate citizen, and it can't come sooner. I believe my parentes feel the same.

"What are your plans this day?"

"Nothing beyond the norm."

We speak The Standard. It's based on the Great Tongue, Latin. The Ancients called it a dead language. We revived it and implemented it in all the realms of Earth.

"I am pleased you are adorned in your favorite color. It highlights the deep scarlet of your hair. It is a lovely reflection of your celebration."

"I appreciate your kind words, Mater. I hoped my choice would delight you."

She smiles at me as her eyes flicker uncomfortably toward the culina. She has exhausted the breadth of her planned dialog. As I dine, she softly clears her throat. I believe she does it because she's uncomfortable with the silence, yet she has no thoughts on how to break it. Sometime in my fourteenth year, I stopped offering assistance.

She clears her throat again and says, "Would you like more pomegranate juice?"

"No, thank you."

Again she clears her throat. "I believe I would like another cup of tea. Do excuse me, Rayne. Please do not think me ill of manners."

I glance at her to offer an approving smile. Frankly, I prefer to be alone instead of listening to her throat.

While I dine, I soak in the surroundings. Wild grass, native plant life, and moss-covered stone cover the grounds. Our villa is nestled in a forest of trees. The Great Oaks, Aspens, and Willows surrounding our villa only allow the slightest bits of sunlight on the interior.

I love the particular arrangement of trees on our grounds. The leaves are beginning to change to the brilliant colors of autumn. I only have one month remaining in this domus, so I will not witness the falling of the final leaf. It's one of the few things I'll miss.

As I swallow the last bites, I notice a pack of wolves entering our grounds. A pup wanders onto the veranda, sniffing the aroma. I reach down to stroke him and say, "Greetings, young one. There is no sustenance here for you. You must learn as your elders have done." As I finish my words, a female wolf approaches. She looks into my eyes, and I gaze into hers.

As if she could respond to my words, I whisper to her. "Salvē. Has your pack already dined this morn? If so, I do hope it was as savory as my own."

She crouches and tilts her head upward and downward. She then rises and nudges her pup forward. For a moment, I think she understood me, but I know it can't be so. I'm not a susurrator—a whisperer. I have no abilities.

Yet, she responded with what looked like a nod. As I watch them leave, my thoughts drift to last night. Though it follows no logic, I allow myself to believe the impossible: I experienced the Luminescence 15 years later than I should have.

2

My heart pounds. My head is light. I force myself to breathe. This isn't panic. It's exhilaration.

They must have witnessed this. I turn toward the culina. My mater stands with her back to me, sipping her tea. My pater is engrossed in his affairs. I should go to them, tell them they have no more need for shame. I push aside my plate and scramble to my feet. The scuffling noise causes my pater to regard me with such a look of disapproval that I lower myself to my chair with a thud. My mater turns to me and lifts a hand, motioning me to stay.

Though their reaction doesn't surprise me, my throat spasms from the suppression of tears. I lower my face to my dish. I decide not to tell them. Maybe they don't deserve to know.

My mater steps onto the veranda and speaks in a rushed whisper. "I see you have not completed your morning fare. Is there anything additional you request?"

"No. I just—the proportion was too grand."

"Very well. I will store the rest for you. Will you spend the day in frivolity or attend Institute?"

"I will see where my feet lead me."

"Then have a wonderful day, dear Rayne. Upon your return this eve, we will celebrate your day of birth with your favorite evening fare."

"I am eager to do so." I offer her the ritual kiss on the cheek, my lips hot with heartache. I wonder if she can feel it.

I trot down the steps. I need to run. I need to forget how my pater responded when I stood. It's nothing new.

I allow my feet to carry me swiftly, dodging the rocks and roots in my path. With each step, my bitterness wanes. I allow the excitement of possibilities to replace it.

A stream of two paces wide lies ahead. I increase my speed and calculate my stride. I crouch, raise my arms above my head, and leap. My legs feel lighter than ever, though I have leapt across it countless times. I land squarely on my feet then throw myself to the ground. I bury my hands in the soil. Alone, amidst the trees and the soothing flow of water, my heart pounds at the anticipation of discovery.

I lie on my back and release a primitive roar. Then I close my eyes and steady the pace of my breath. I need an encounter with another creature to confirm this, but first I need to calm down.

I study the sounds of nature. No creature is present. I hear something else. It's the sound of stirring air. I'm no longer alone.

Before I can react, I hear laughter. I know that laugh. It's male, it's friendly, and it belongs to my only comrade.

I wipe the soil from my hands and hop to my feet. "Rafe! How long have you been here?"

"Long enough to hear your fierce roar. I reckon you frighten all the creatures in this quadrant of forest."

He grins at me from his zephyr-mobile. It's opaque white and made of fiberglass and aluminum alloy. Whenever he rides in the fullness of the sun, it shimmers with a warmth to match his smile. My eyes drift to his leathery bottoms, accenting the musculature of his long legs. He wears a gray textile top with sleeves that extend to his elbows. The soft material clings to his torso. I feel heat rise to my face when I realize my eyes have lingered too long.

He hops to the ground, leaving his zephyr-mobile in its neutral setting, hovering one meter above the ground. He strokes a hand through his thick hair which hangs just above his shoulders. It's dyed the blood-orange rays of the sun low on the horizon. His thick brows broadcast his natural color of cinnamon brown. His broad nose and full lips enhance it.

"I hope your parentes do not see you like this—unless you mean to irk your mater by soiling your attire. Per viam, a special day of birth to you."

His tawny-brown eyes sparkle in the radiance of his smile. No other person ever looks at me like he does. He smiles at me like he means it.

I brush the remnants of dirt from my hands but ignore the smears on my top. In the presence of any other person I would feel improper. In front of him, I feel like myself.

"Thank you, Rafe. As for my appearance, you know it is the least of my concerns."

"This is why I adore you the most."

I know he's being facetious, but his words make my cheeks flush. "Ah, Rafe, I know you only mean to mock me."

"Not at all."

Our eyes meet, and we stand in silence. I try to think of something clever to say. He speaks first.

"I meant to offer my good wishes before you left this morn. I have just come from your villa. Your mater did not know where I might find you. So, I consider myself lucky to have discovered you…like this," he laughs.

"What would you do without me to fill your daily quotient of humor?"

"I would shrivel in boredom, I suppose." He brushes his

hand over his beardless face and tilts his head in wonder. "In all matter of seriousness, do tell me. What brings you about so early this morn? Surely you do not wish to attend Institute. Or is this your intention, spending the day romping in the soil?"

"I have not yet decided," I laugh. "Perhaps I will go for a swim."

"I envy you. Working on my mural is causing me too much stress these days. The elements have not been cooperating. I am on the verge of begging an aerisma to quiet the wind while I work. The constant blowing of loose soil is a plague on my wet paints."

Rafe is an artist. It's his chosen position in life. He paints and sculpts, and he's exquisite. The largest of his sculptures sits in the main plaza at Institute. Each time I go, it reminds me I have a comrade while among so many who are not.

His ability is emovis. He can read the emotions of others as if they speak them with words. It's immoral to do so intrusively. Emoves tend to be passive about their own emotions. Rafe expresses his through his art. When first I met him, I thought he was as dry and dull as my pater. It didn't take long to see Rafe is much less so. Perhaps it's because he's artistic and my pater is not.

"Think of the dust and debris as a textural accent to make your mural sparkle."

"Ha! Yes, well I can always count on you to lighten my

mood. Now, as for your plans for midday, am I to hope you will meet me at our usual place?"

"Of course I will, Rafe."

"Well then, I will bring an extra blanket for you in the event of your swim-attired arrival. I would hate for you to catch a chill."

I linger in the warmth of his smile. I wish he could spend this day with me. His presence would make the hours pass much more agreeably. Other than midday fare with him, I will spend it alone.

Alone. I've ignored why I'm here in the first place. Suddenly, I'm anxious for him to leave.

"You seem suddenly agitated. Am I usurping your time?"

"Far from it, Rafe. Why would you say that?"

"Well, I know you too well to think it is due to this day, however brightly clad you are."

I want to tell him the source of my joy. I trust he will believe me, but first, I must believe it myself. "Actually, there is something I must do. And the winds are still. You had best be off before it changes."

He narrows his discerning eyes and says, "If you insist on playing a game of secrets, I will allow it…for now. But I will expect a full report of your morn when I see you at midday."

"You will be the first human soul with whom I share the details."

"Human?" He waits for me to respond, but I only offer a

smile. "Well if you insist on being coy, I have no choice but to wait in wonder."

He takes a step toward me and lightly rests his hands on my shoulders. He leans forward to kiss my forehead, and my nose brushes his neck. The aroma of juniper berries and lilac permeates my senses.

"It appears you have been at the task of mixing paints this morn," I find myself saying, cringing at my awkward statement.

He lowers his head and whispers in my ear, "You know me well. I was in want of more shades of purple." He lowers his hands from my arms, kisses me on the cheek and says, "Farewell, Rayne. I will see you at midday."

"Farewell, Rafe."

He takes a running stride then leaps onto his zephyr-mobile. He winks and smiles, and silently I watch him leave.

I feel odd standing in the forest, my eyes lingering on the traces of his departure. I force myself to run. It reignites the excitement within me of a possible new reality.

Several meters ahead, I spot a doe drinking from a brook. My feet lead me almost too swiftly to support my weight. I stumble from sheer anticipation and stop when I'm a few paces from her. Her ears twitch in the dim light of the wooded morn. I've only slightly startled her.

My lips part to release my panting breath, and I whisper, "Salvē, Doe. Is the water delightfully crisp this morn?"

She pauses in her drink, her nose skirting the surface of the water. She turns to me and dips her head upward and downward.

"Do you understand me?" I whisper.

When she bobs her head, I know she answers, yes. She studies me while I consider what else to say to prove it to myself.

I retreat a few steps, lift a wondering finger, and extend my arm. "If you comprehend my words, Doe, I bid you to demonstrate it now. Please touch your nose to my finger."

She complies without pause.

My laugh sounds more like a shriek as it echoes in the quiet forest. "How is this so?"

She does nothing. I have asked the wrong form of question. "If you do not think me too brash, might I hold your hoof in my hand?"

She bobs her head again then lifts a leg. I catch it in my hands and slide my palm under it. It's brittle yet soft, cold, yet thriving on the warmth of her life.

"It would seem I am somehow a susurrator. Do you agree, Doe?" I say, releasing her hoof from my grip.

She nods and offers a quick lick on my nose with her tongue. She blinks and places her nose on the tip of mine. We stand there nose to nose, and I can feel her breath, moist and warm and comforting.

"I *have* become a susurrator, and you are the second creature with whom I share it. Thank you for accommodating me," I smile, patting her on her elegant neck.

She tilts her head downward then turns to the brook for another drink. I leave her to it, running through the forest and belting an exultant yell.

I leap and hop over rocks and shrubs. The farther I run the happier I become. It's a foreign feeling, and I never want it to end.

"*Susurrator*," I shout to the birds in the trees and the insects scurrying beneath my path. I squeal and laugh and shout in the Old Tongue of English, "Today's my birthday, and I've received the coolest present of all. I'm a Whisperer!"

I run and shout in The Standard, to whatever creature might hear me, "This is the day of my birth, and I am reborn!"

The sound of a derisive chuckle quiets me. I know who it is. It's the last voice I want to hear right now.

"If you look to your left, you will spot a savage beast in her natural habitat."

I cringe at the words, but I force myself not to respond or look at the source of the taunt. It's what he wants. His name is Jhonis. Of all my age peers, I loathe him the most. The sound of his voice saturates my pores with irritation.

"If you look closer, you might detect the slightest semblance of joy on her Sape countenance. My apologies. It appears to have been fleeting. She is a simple creature. Also, I advise you not to meet her gaze. Doing so might provoke the savage beast."

The next voice I hear belongs to a female. "I dare say, upon our arrival, she appeared to be in a state of good cheer. I wonder why. It is so uncharacteristic."

Her name is Diamond. She once rivaled Jhonis in her cruelty toward me. Over the past year, it has waned. At first I attributed it to her missing her frater. When he came of age, he moved to a new province. Now I believe she simply lost interest in infantile behavior. She rarely speaks to me directly. She behaves as though it pains her to acknowledge my presence. I prefer it this way. I wish Jhonis would do the same.

They hover two meters above ground in Jhonis's zephyr-craft. Its fiberglass and aluminum alloy body is painted yellow with brown splotches. It emulates the great Giraffe which once roamed Earth. It seats two, and as far as I know, it has only ever carried one passenger: Diamond.

Jhonis steers the craft closer to me then rests it idly under his command. His pale-pink hair hangs limply in his face. His matching, pointy chin hair seems exaggerated as he peers down at me.

"It would appear our Sape here has been making merriment in the soil like the pink, squealing pigs of old. Diamond, recall the transmission we viewed at Institute our prime year? Does she not remind you of those pink beasts? All Sape here needs is to replace the blue with the color of swine flesh, and I would not be able to tell her from them."

As he laughs, his gray eyes narrow in provocation. I stare back at him with an unwavering grimace then turn to seek the green eyes of Diamond. She refuses to meet my gaze as if she cannot tolerate the act. She tosses her shoulder-length, green-streaked hair to shield her face from my view.

I refuse to allow Jhonis to ruin my day. I need both of them to leave. "I must say, with each unintelligent word you waste, you run the risk of arriving at Institute late. It would behoove you to set your craft in motion and leave me in the peace of your absence."

His face tenses with irritation at the failure of his insults. He releases a paltry attempt at a sneer and says, "A pity I cannot offer you transport. Even if I commanded a larger craft, I still would not, lest your Sape filth stain the interior. I dare say no horse would carry you in your current state. You must run, lest you find *yourself* tardy. Though a beast has no concern for such decorum."

"There is nothing to which I will be tardy. I will not be attending Institute this day. So, you are wrong, Jhonis. It is a concept at which you are well-versed."

"Allow me to guess. Judging by your asinine attempt at donning a cheerful color, I presume this is your day of birth. How fitting your attire has become as sullied as your personality. Or do I have it wrong? What say you on this, Diamond?"

"Of course we know it is her day of birth, Jhonis," Diamond deigns to confirm.

"Ah, yes. I was right. Then allow me to offer my most sincere of greetings. May your day be as tainted as your attire."

"Jhonis, I am bored of this exchange," Diamond says in a tone dripping with exaggerated indifference.

"As am I," I say. "It is you, Jhonis, who soils this day. Seeing the back of you will improve my mood tenfold, I assure you."

"Well then, allow me to offer you my final words on this pathetic day of yours. May you pass this day in mud as grimy as your wit. Until the morrow, Sape."

He sends his zephyr-craft in motion. As I choke on the echo of his grating laugh, I realize my hands have clenched into fists. I relax them and expel his negative energy through several deep breaths. I clear my mind of the anger he always elicits in me. It's useless to dwell. His words don't matter. He's nothing to me. The brief interaction with the two of them will not ruin my day.

My feet lead me through a cluster of Great Oaks. I increase my speed, navigating the trunks with ease. One with a low-hanging branch stands a few meters ahead. Beyond it lies a clearing. Without thinking, I leap.

I grab onto the branch and pull myself onto it. My legs propel me upward, and I cling to a higher one. I climb without pause, navigating those which can bear my weight.

I reach the crown of the Great Oak and balance my footing, distributing my center so the branches support me. When my head and shoulders clear the canopy, I melt at the breathtaking view. In all directions is a maze of greens and browns of the vast forest. I have witnessed this many times, but now it's even more magnificent.

In the distance lies an angular structure of glass and concrete. Far removed from the hub of destruction, it's one of the great structures which survived the wars of the Ancients. It was once a museum for visual art. Now it's a place of knowledge for subordinate citizens, our Institute. It's where we discuss the past so we don't repeat their mistakes. It's also where we decide our path when we come of age.

Before this morn, there was not much I could do to be of use in a colony of 200. This day changes everything. Now I have purpose. When I relocate to a new colony, they will only ever know me as a susurrator.

The rustling of leaves and swaying of branches startles me. A visitor is near. I watch as he swings his small, furry body through the branches and perches near me. He clutches an apple in his grip and waves his long tail in triumph.

"Salvē, Monkey."

He releases a high-pitched shriek as he offers his fruit to me. "No, thank you. I have already consumed fare this morn."

He utters softer shrieks, raises the apple above his head, then lowers it to take a bite. As he dines on the fruit, I notice a shadow passing over the canopy. I look up in search of the source and see a master eagle soaring above us.

To say this great beast of the sky is the largest of flying creatures, does nothing to boast its size. It's proportional to a horse, with a wingspan that surpasses the height of a Weeping Willow. It's massive yet elegant, and no one has ever mounted one.

Some believe the master eagle is the result of ancient scientific experiments on the bald eagle. There's no known proof of this. I believe Mother Earth yearned for the return of her grandest creatures and accomplished it through evolution of the bald eagle.

"How splendid it would be if Master Eagle could hear my whisper." I turn to the monkey, but he's gone. All that's left is the ruffling of leaves and branches in his hasty descent.

I return my focus to the sky and imagine what it would be like if the master eagle could hear my beckoning. No susurrator has ever come close enough.

As its path circles above me, I sense its essence—*his* essence. He must be scouting his meal. I imagine stroking the silky feathers and soaring through the clouds, far above everyone I know. Though I know he won't hear me, I close my eyes. A smile creeps to my lips, and I whisper, "Fly to me, Master Eagle. Carry me from this place."

When I open my eyes, his beak is pointed downward. As he appears to fly toward me, I imagine he heard me.

He must be searching for prey. I sink lower on the

branches. His eyes seem to be fixed on me. I hold my breath and remain still. He dives closer, swallowing me in the shadow of his greatness.

He flies straight to me as if I'm his prey. I descend to a lower branch, the sound of my shriek ringing in my ears. I scramble down a few more branches, terrified.

I hold my breath. He levels his path. A mighty wind parts the leaves, forcing the branches to bow in the wake of his massive, flapping wings.

I'm exposed.

His piercing, golden eyes stare down at me. His talons hover above me. I think he means to grab me. I force myself to remain still.

He lowers himself, flapping his wings as he hovers in the clearing. His body and wings devour the open space. He stares at me, tilting his head up and down…almost as if he's nodding.

He drifts closer, within my reach. My fright shifts to wonder. I don't think, I act.

I lift a timid hand and graze his silky feathers. He lowers himself further, and I extend my arm. I stroke his plumy chest, and he ruffles his neck feathers. I catch his scent. He smells of the winds and the Earth. He smells of solitude and freedom.

My lips part, and I whisper, "Salvē, Master Eagle. You heard me?"

He dips his head as if he's motioning, yes.

"May I stroke your beak?"

He sinks so his beak meets my extended hand. As I offer a few strokes, I confess, "I long to soar with you, Master Eagle."

The tip of his beak grazes my hand when he turns from me. He presents his back and jerks his beak to the sky. I understand him. He's granting my wish. I climb onto his broad back and wrap my arms around him.

I close my eyes, and then I drink the wind.

3

As the setting sun nuzzles the horizon, I'm mesmerized. I've witnessed it from a great height, but never before like this.

The crisp wind caresses my face, and I long to remain up here, flying and free. I have no desire to return to land, but decorum compels me. I stroke the silky back of the master eagle, cherishing the final moments of our flight.

Even up here, I recognize the arrangement of trees of my grounds. I whisper to him to carry me to a cluster of Willows on the perimeter. He descends low enough for me to jump. When I land, my legs feel as light as air.

I sink onto a bench under the oldest of Weeping Willows.

As the drooping branches dance in the winds of his departure, I regret my choice to return to land.

I force my eyes from the sky. I stroke the bench of concrete, metal, and glass. I wish to caress the wind instead. The surface I sit on is hard and lifeless. I long for the master eagle's warmth.

I trace my fingers over letters engraved in the concrete: DIA. This bench belongs to my mater. It has been in her familia for generations. Her ancestors collected the materials from a place once called an airport.

Such places no longer exist. From database records, we know why. Centuries before The Rebirth Period, a great war devastated the Earth. We know it as World War X. It endured for a hundred years. It was initiated when all ports of air travel were bombed by an organization which meant to destroy the civil world. They succeeded.

I flinch from the knowledge of it. I'm too ecstatic to dwell on destruction. This is a day for celebration.

This day I have realized a new means of air travel. It has come to me alone, and I want everyone to know.

I open my mouth to shout to whatever creatures might hear when I notice my mater in the distance. Though she has returned from her day of duty, I can see she's not finished.

She crouches next to a withering rose bush, her hands poised above it. She lifts her face to the sky and closes her eyes. Even from this distance I can detect the fluttering of her lashes.

I've witnessed her performing her ability a few times. This is the part I enjoy the most. I study her and the bush, hypnotized by the serenity of her purpose. She's a floresca—a flourisher of botanic life.

I watch as the thorns transform from the brittleness of death to deep brown. She removes her hand before tiny buds appear. It's too late in the season for the bush to flower.

When she opens her eyes, my impulse is to run to her to share my own ability. I make a few strides when my pater steps onto the veranda. At this hour, he's complete with his own duty. My pulse increases from anticipation. In a few moments, they will both rejoice with me.

A soft swooshing of air makes me halt. I turn around to see Rafe on his zephyr-mobile, his slouching posture and somber eyes directed at me.

Guilt replaces my glee. Up there with the master eagle, I forgot about him and our midday fare.

"Here you are, Rayne. I find myself dejected yet relieved to see you suffered no ill fate this day."

"Rafe! Please forgive me and pardon my absence. I merely…something occurred which…" I struggle to find the right words to explain my fantastical experience.

"You have no need to pardon yourself for my benefit."

"No, I *do.* And once I explain, not only will you understand the cause of my rudeness, you will pardon it."

He hops to the ground, his curiosity silencing his disappointment. "Has this anything to do with your odd behavior earlier?"

"It does, and I will tell you everything."

He's about to respond, but his focus drifts behind me. His eyes narrow in annoyance. "However, I fear it must wait. I believe your pater wishes to speak with you."

I turn to see my pater striding toward us in his usual demeanor. It does not suggest pleasantries.

"Sir Rafe," he says with a terse nod. "I see you have come to my domus thrice in one day in search of my filia. Now you have found her. Consequently, there is no further reason for you to remain on my premises. Please depart at once, lest I be forced to regard you with discourtesy."

"A fair eve to you, Sir Roman. Since you have already failed at a proper greeting, I assure you, your discourtesy only mildly offends."

"You dare instruct me on matters of decorum?"

Rafe glances at me with a wink then turns to my pater and says, "I'm here because I had to know why your daughter didn't come to our daily lunch."

I struggle to stifle a laugh at his blatant insertion of the Old Tongue of English. My pater flinches from his irritation of it. I can tell Rafe wishes to say more, but he doesn't. He won't push further without allowing my pater his retort. Moments like this make me wish such restraint were not ingrained in our species.

The relations of Rafe and my pater have always been contentious. I've never known the source of it. I can only assume it's due to Rafe being three years my senior.

"How dare you address me in an uncivilized tongue. You will show me the respect I am due."

"You misunderstand my intent, kind sir," Rafe says, his smile saturated with perfect social grace. It's fake. I know what his real smile looks like.

"I believe I understand you perfectly."

"Sir Roman, let us not soil this day for Rayne."

"Now you accuse me of besmirching the day of birth of *my* filia? It is you who does so by your impertinence."

"I beg of you to tend to your manners, Sir Roman, so I may complete my thought." A curt smile creeps to his lips from his irritation, but he forces his eyes to soften with civility. "I have come to confirm the well-being of *our* Rayne. If you take offense to my use of an Old Tongue, do accept my apology. I merely inserted it for her benefit. You know she delights in such things."

"Do not instruct me on matters of her fancy as if I am ignorant of them. As for you confirming her state of health, you have already obtained your evidence of it. I have tolerated your presence more than propriety deems, so kindly remove yourself from my premises."

"Roman!"

My mater's admonishing voice startles me. She marches toward us, her face set with a sternness I rarely see. It's only ever directed at my pater and only within the privacy of our domus.

"Kindly restore your demeanor to one of cordiality, Roman. Your manner of speaking is below the respect due our guest."

"Sapphire, were you not ignorant of the details of our conversation, you would know I am not at fault for my words."

"I heard all, Roman."

My pater contorts his face in wounded pride. His lips quiver as he considers his retort. Since Rafe came to see me and not them, I decide it's my turn to speak.

"Rafe, as I stated, I hope you will pardon me for missing our midday fare."

"Of course I do."

"Mirificus. Now I have a request. Would you care to dine with us this eve? Surely Pater will not protest since this is my day of birth." I regard my pater with all the feigned innocence I can muster. His eyes widen in protest, but he bunches his lips and remains silent. It would be rude of him to oppose.

"Thank you for your offer, Rayne, but I do not wish to subject Sir Roman to further emotional strife by my presence. Would you accompany me on a stroll instead?"

"As my pater will inform you himself, your presence would

only bring delight. Tell him, Pater. Otherwise we may start to think of you as ill-natured." Something about flying high and free with the master eagle has made me bold. I've never spoken to him like this.

My pater turns from me with such force that he looks like a child in a fit. My mater answers for him. "Truly, it is no bother, Rafe. I have yet to go to the Harvesting Center for meats, so I will buy enough for us all. Roman, please tell Rafe he is more than welcome to join our table this eve."

She places a hand on my pater's shoulder, and he opens his mouth just wide enough to say, "Yes, join us."

"It is settled," I say. "You will dine with us."

"I suppose now, it would be rude of me not to accept. Thank you. You honor me in your grace, Sir Roman."

My pater ignores the innuendo. Before he has a chance to ruin the mood, I decide this is the perfect moment to share my news.

"There is something I wish to say." I pause, unsure how to begin. I breathe the cool air and compose myself. I close my eyes and remember what it was like to soar. I recite the words in my head then speak them aloud. *"It* happened to me last night."

I open my eyes, expecting them to understand my meaning. They only stare at me with curiosity.

"Must I repeat it? I said *it* happened to me."

"What *it?"* Rafe asks.

"Yes, dear Rayne," my mater says. "What are you referring to? What happened?"

"Have you taken ill? If so, I will summon a medicum at once."

"I assure you I am well of mind, body, and spirit, Pater. In truth," I add with a smile, "it is a statement which has never been truer for me." I pause, unable to contain my excitement. When my mouth widens in a grin, they look at me like I've gone mad.

"Rayne, if you toy with us any further, I fear I will burst." Forgetting himself, Rafe places his hands on my shoulders and caresses them.

The sound of a clearing throat startles me. I retreat a few steps from his reach. I notice my parentes exchanging glances. Neither of them speaks, but my pater grunts to express his disdain. It's a sound I know well.

"Do proceed, Rayne," my mater says.

"Forgive the theatrics. It is just…I am at a loss for how to start."

"Well then, the beginning seems like the best place to me," Rafe says with a wink.

"Very well." I bunch my lips as I take several deep breaths. Then I hear myself speak. "The Luminescence came to me last night, and before I left this morn, I discovered my ability. I am a susurrator."

I don't know how I expected them to react. I don't know

what I expected them to say. I only thought it would be *something.* Instead they all gape at me, their eyes accusing me of lies.

My mater is the first to end the silence. "Dear Rayne, while I am curious as to what experience of wonder must have occurred, you know what you describe is impossible."

"I know, but I *am* a susurrator," I declare, a ball of disappointment burning my throat. Yet, I do not blame her. It *is* supposed to be impossible.

"Rayne," my pater begins with a tone I know well. It's as if to tell me I know nothing because I'm tainted. "You know your mater is entirely correct in her statement. You know she speaks fact."

"Perhaps you should share with us why you are convinced this is true. Surely you have cause to believe this. You are no fabricator of tales." Though Rafe smiles, his eyes reveal his opinion. He doesn't believe me either.

"Dear Rayne, is it possible your impending status has influenced your dreams, and the stress of it all has confused you about what is real?"

"Impending status? What is real? I know what is real, Mater."

"Please, Rayne. While I cannot pretend to understand the prospect of coming of age as Unregistered, I *do* understand your need to belong—"

"I do not like your inference, Mater, and I wholly reject

it," I say my eyes stinging from tears. Though I cannot fault her or any of them, their disbelief still wounds me. "I do not fear my impending status. In fact, I long for it. I long for the day I quit this domus for good."

I regret the words the moment I speak them. Though it's how I feel, I shouldn't have said it. My mater regards me with such shock, it's obvious how much I've upset her. I didn't think it was possible. I believed she longed for my departure as much as I did.

"Allow me to make a suggestion," Rafe begins. "It is quite simple—if you are not opposed, Rayne. Why not show us? Then we can resolve the matter at once. I do not wish for you to think I question the veracity, but surely you see why my suggestion is best?"

"I think it inappropriate to demand such a thing, Rafe," my mater says. "She can simply describe the cause of her conviction. Then we can determine the truth of it—what actually transpired."

"I concur," my pater huffs. "There are no creatures in our midst, Rafe. Would you have us stand here in wait for nothing more than humiliation? Describe your encounter, Rayne, so we might proceed with the rest of this eve." He behaves as though the exchange is too exasperating for him to bear.

"I am comforted by your empathy, Pater," I say with all the spite I can muster. "I assure you I will be free from whatever humiliation you think I will endure. What I declare is no matter of desire. It is a matter of fact. Yet, I will do as you bid me and tell you everything."

I begin with the wolves. I study the reactions of my parentes when I recount my cause for seeking their attention this morn. I look for signs of regret, but there are none.

I describe my encounters with the doe and the monkey. I can't tell whether they believe me or if they think I'm simply describing what I've witnessed a susurrator do. I haven't convinced them. I realize I have to omit my flight with the master eagle. Telling them would be too much.

I wander to the Weeping Willow and brush my hand along its leaves. I wait for their response, but no one speaks. One of them must. I don't care who. The silence is intolerable. I don't look at any of them for fear their eyes show pity. I stare at my feet, and I imagine the sensation of the wind on my soles.

My mater clears her throat.

I cringe.

I feel heat rising to my cheeks. I have no more words to say which will convince them. I decide to listen to Rafe. I'll prove everything I say is true.

"Since none of you has anything else to say, you will watch." Without waiting for them to respond, I turn and run.

Several paces ahead is a cluster of Great Pines. I run to the nearest one, grab onto a low branch, and climb. I don't look down to see if they follow. I climb higher and faster. I hear them calling to me. I have no words for them. I will show them.

I reach the canopy and search the sky. I know there's little chance he's still near, but I have to try. I hear the ruffling of leaves. I don't look to see who it is, but I know it must be Rafe.

"Rayne, what are you doing?" The worry in his voice is evident. "Look about. There is no monkey present. You have nothing to prove. We do not doubt you believe what you say. I know how much you desire it to be so. Please understand it to be a matter of coincidence. None of us can nor will hold you at fault for it."

Coincidence.

I ignore him and focus on the sky, whispering to the horizon, "Come to me, Master Eagle, so I might soar with you."

I feel a hand on my ankle and fingers gripping the fabric of my bottoms.

"Master eagle? No creature could hear you at such a distance, *especially* a master eagle. This you already know …Rayne!"

Rafe's hand grips my calf.

"Very well, Rayne. Even if what you speak is truth, the great beasts of the sky have never heeded the call of a susurrator. You know this to be fact, so please, Rayne, cease this."

I ignore the sound of his voice. Instead, I imagine I'm soaring, the feel of feathers and the mighty beat of wings.

Again I whisper.

A dark speck moves in the distance. It grows larger with each syllable I utter. He has heard me.

I feel nothing save the wind. I'm lost in the sky and the form which grows larger with each word of my beckoning. His white-capped head becomes whiter with each stroke of his wings and his beak more defined in the light of the setting sun.

He's close now, and I know his eyes are directed at me. I part my lips in a smile. I know I don't need to whisper again. He comes to me.

I no longer care if Rafe or my parentes are watching. The master eagle approaches with a swiftness which I long to embrace.

The branches submit to the might of his wings. I breathe his scent on the wind as he slows his approach. I extend my hand. I can almost touch him.

"*Rayne.* Get down! He thinks we are prey."

I feel Rafe's hands on my waist. I mount a higher branch to free myself from his grip. I shift forward and balance my footing.

The master eagle presents his back to me, and I leap. I wrap my arms around him and bury my face in his feathers. When a hand clutches my ankle, I kick my foot to free it.

"Fly with me, Master Eagle."

He spreads his wings. The wind floods my pores.

A persistent voice grows fainter.

We climb higher, away from the ground, away from the doubt. He carries me to the clouds at a great speed, before leveling his path to the setting sun.

Exhilaration devours me, yet I find myself searching for the Great Oak. I see the tiny form of Rafe staring up at me. My heart beats in triumph when the head and shoulders of my parentes appear next to him. They are all there, watching me.

The farther we soar, the smaller they become. They are tiny specks amidst a sea of greens, reds, and brown. I have forgotten anger and hurt. As I soar above them, my heart pounds with the force of the wind, because I've left them no room for doubt.

4

You must tell no one. None save us four must know.

These are the words which plague me as I lie awake. My pater spoke them, but they are the sentiments of them all. Though their faces were filled with wonder, they voiced only warnings. For the first time since I've known him, Rafe was in accord with my pater.

No one must know any of it: the Luminescence, my ability, or the master eagle. My pater forbids it all.

Why must I say nothing? It will cause too much confusion and chaos in my colony? I can't believe anyone too feeble of mind to accept it. I don't know why this happened, but we should celebrate it. Instead, my parentes want me to act like nothing has changed, because they're afraid of what's happening to me. And they obviously care more about what others think than letting me feel normal for the first time in years.

I refuse to lie awake in despair. I focus on the crickets singing their late-night song. Each night, they lull me to my dreams. I shift in my pod, nestling in the silky fabric, but it's no use. The charm of the crickets has no effect. I can't fall asleep.

I need something to distract me. Since I didn't attend Institute and missed my favorite discussion, *Secret Journals of the Early Homo Praestans*, I decide to read on the topic. I reach for my holodigit on my table and slip it in place. I tap my index finger to my thumb, and a field of light appears before me. When I tap again, my catalog of early Homo praestans scribes appears. I wave my index finger to scroll through the list and pause on the journal of Lev Nikolayevich Tolstoy. I stare blankly at words in the Old Tongue of Russian. My irritation prevents me from focusing.

I wave my hand and scroll through the list again. This time I pause on Socrates. He's one of the earliest of our species. I believe I'll find the solace I need in the wisdom of his philosophy. I wave my fingers as if I'm flipping through pages born of the sacred tree. With a flicker of a finger, the motion stops.

As I nestle into my pod and read a few lines, the light from the field suddenly becomes too intense for my eyes. The randomness of it startles me. I remove my device from my fingers and toss it onto my table. My stomach aches from the motion. I press my hand to my abdomen to ease the sensation.

I focus on the darkness, breathing deeply to lessen the pain. I try to distract myself. I imagine the master eagle carrying me across oceans which I've never seen. I imagine discovering another person like me.

A feeling of dizziness strikes me, and I forget my thoughts. I roll to my side and curl into a ball. I clutch my stomach now full of acid and bloat.

My skin moistens from no incitation of heat. My mouth waters, my throat tightens, and I know I have little time to reach the safety of my chamber wash room.

I fling myself from my pod and try to steady myself on quivering legs. I force my feet forward, wincing from the sensation of spinning.

I reach my wash room threshold. My vision is blurred, but I don't need to see. I extend a shaky hand to lift the lid of the latrine. I sink to my knees, stare into the depths of the watery sanctuary, and empty the contents of my stomach.

When there is nothing more to release, I slump to my side and rest my cheek on the soothingly cold floor. I dare not move. I *can't* move. I know I've experienced this, and I wonder why it's happening again. I wonder if I ever heard anyone describe their night following the Luminescence. But I know no one ever has. There was nothing ever to tell.

This isn't supposed to be happening. Something is wrong …or perhaps something is right.

As I lie quivering on the floor, I remind myself I've never heard of anyone else summoning a master eagle. My ability is powerful, so the effects must be too.

I close my eyes, and the room spins. I roll to my stomach and press my forehead to the floor. My panting breath echoes in my ears. My body shakes, and my teeth grind with a grating force. I can't control it. It's useless to fight it.

My body is dripping with sweat. I feel heavy, like I'm sinking into the floor. I writhe in a state of dizzying pain. This time is more intense. I feel as though I will die.

I focus on my breath. My stomach hardens with acid, but there's no release. I grind my teeth, clutching my stomach for a relief which doesn't come. I shiver and writhe. I moan and grunt. I want to cry but I can't.

Something is wrong. This is wrong. I struggle to think, but I can only feel: the garments clinging to my flesh, the grinding of my teeth, the hard mound of my stomach, the spasms of my muscles causing my body to contract. Shrouded in darkness and misery, I lie helpless, wishing for the stillness of death.

A maddening swirl of images appears. I try to make sense of them, but all I can decipher is a blur of greens and browns anchoring brighter splotches of color.

I focus on the visions, burying myself in them. As the dizziness subsides, I feel heavy and calm. My breathing steadies, my muscles relax, and the colors fade to black.

5

A pale light shines through the refurbished pieces of stain and clear glass. I can't remember my dreams save the nightmare in which I longed for death. When I feel my body pressed against the floor of my wash room and my sleep garments clinging to my flesh, I know it wasn't a dream. It was real.

I have faint memories of swirling colors before sleep claimed me, but I can't grasp them long enough to understand them. They're just flashes of imagery, fleeting and vague.

Then something occurs to me which sends the heat of dread to my face. I know what this must be. The Luminescence returned to reclaim its gift. I can think of no other explanation for the night I endured and how I feel now. If this is true, never again will I fly. My new existence has vanished as suddenly as it came.

I curl into a fetal position in physical and mental anguish. I shield my face from the soft light of dawn. It's too serene for how I feel.

I need to release my anguish through tears, but they don't come. I can't change what is. I also can't languish in denial and spend the day hiding in my chamber.

It's *dies da Vinci*, and I'm obligated to attend Institute. The idea of returning sickens me as much as the acid in my stomach. I want to tell them all—show them all—I'm like them. As I loosen my grip on my stomach, I remind myself there may no longer be a thing to declare.

Even though I hope I'm wrong, it doesn't change much. I can't tell anyone, simply because my parentes are afraid and too concerned with what people think.

I force myself from the floor and drift through my morning routine. It feels like hours have passed when I'm ready to leave my chamber. I lift a hand to deactivate my threshold when I hear voices. I press the button, and they silence, but I sense their stifled breath. My parentes have been discussing me. Of this I have no doubt.

I fill my lungs on anticipation and expel them with resolve. If I tell them of my night, they'll be relieved to know everything is back to normal. It'll also renew their disappointment in me. I don't know which is worse: their forbidding me to declare my ability, or their impending reaction that once again, my existence has failed them.

I have no choice. I have to tell them the truth.

The first face I see in the corridor meets me with eyes filled with solemnity and grace. I force myself to smile as I consider how to say it.

"My filia, Rayne. How does this new morn greet you?"

My pater offers a genuine smile. I forgot what it looks like on his face. It tortures me. After I tell him, I doubt I'll see it again.

I focus on the row of Aspens and hear myself answer, "It greets me with torment, Pater."

"Torment? Why should it be so? There is no cause for it. I understand your desire to share with everyone, but please do not consider your latent ability forfeit. While you are not permitted to perform it, you may rest sound knowing you still possess it. Rejoice in your ability in secret. Allow the private knowledge alone to soothe your soul."

His words enrage me, and I almost forget there may be no secret to keep. The way his eyes wrinkle at the crease and the corners of his mouth twitch in resolve, he thinks he has spoken infinite wisdom.

I tighten my jaw and bunch my lips, ready to spill the truth if only to see his pretentious warmth crumble in a sea of disappointment. It's been a single day. He'll remember the sensation with ease.

My anger towards him clouds my judgment. I forget myself and all I meant to say as my mouth forms words I shouldn't say. "What an awkward occurrence for you to greet me this morn, Pater, seeing as you have not done so in a matter of fifteen years. You wish for me to rejoice in my ability in secret? Your words are an insult. Your pretentious greeting is an insult. Everything about you this morn is an insult. I wish for you to return to your usual manner of regarding me—with apathy at best—because I can assure you of this. I will never tolerate your demand. So, tend to your duty, Pater, and leave me in the peace of your customary coldness."

His face becomes slack as if my words physically struck him. His lips quiver as he considers a retort, but he can find nothing to say in response.

So I continue. "However, before you do so, I will inform you of something. If my words offend you, the blame lies entirely on your head. You have proven you care more for what others think than how I feel. I am starting to think you want me to be hated. You certainly do not care if I am. All you care about is my coming of age and leaving this colony so you can finally be free of me. And I will remind you that once I do come of age, I will be under no obligation to comply with your demand."

His eyes widen in shock and his mouth twitches. He contorts his face in confusion and utter surprise. My own is tense with defiance.

"You speak to me with such—"

"A pleasant day, Pater."

I brush past him, down the Aspen-lined corridor. When I enter the culina, I'm not surprised to see my mater feigning an unnatural interest in the bottom of her vessel.

"Good day to you, Mater." With a slight frown and pursing of my lips, I'm daring her to admonish me.

"I am proud of you, Rayne."

Her words strike me with a force which I didn't expect. I don't know what to do or say. I find myself drifting to the table, dazed by her words. I lift the utensil to my mouth. My throat is too tight to swallow as she continues.

"I know you were overcome with joy and thoughts of future possibilities, and we marred it for you. I beg your forgiveness."

I think the throbbing of my head has prevented me from hearing her right. I fumble to form words and hear myself releasing sputters of breath instead.

For the first time, she rescues me from my awkward silence and says, "We will speak later regarding the details, but before you depart, I wish you to know my opinion. While you cannot be expected to refrain from the display of your new ability, I am sure you can appreciate what I must say."

She pauses and sits across from me. She places her hands

on the table and laces her fingers. I watch the fluttering of her lashes as she stares at her hands. When she looks up, I feel awkward for staring at her, so I lower my face to my dish.

"Dear Rayne, this is a unique situation. We must use discretion until we speak with the Board about registering you. We do not yet know how it will work, since this is…an anomaly. This is why no one can know. What if the Board does not wish it? You must forgive your pater and me for being too overwhelmed to explain last night."

My mouthful almost catches in my throat at the simplicity of it. They merely need to register me with the Board first. It makes so much sense. I almost feel guilty for not allowing my pater to respond. He might have told me had I not provoked him so much.

"The Board. Of course. I understand now. I thought you meant indefinitely. Though I must ask, why was this not the first sentiment Pater shared with me?"

"He has never understood the concept of imparting essential facts before touting his opinions. Also, you stunned him. You have never spoken to him in that manner. But worry not. He will recover. Until then, I hope you can spend this day in the peace which you deserve."

I can find no words to say in response, so I take another bite and chew.

"I thought if a creature should enter our grounds, you might display your ability for me. I would be honored to witness it."

Her words cause my stomach to flip. When I meet her eyes, my heart melts. Her smile radiates with a beauty I believed faded long ago. Once I confess what happened last night…I am not ready for that.

"Pater has a different opinion. Is he aware you oppose him?"

"He knows. Please understand he thinks he is being cautious. While I agree with his intentions, I do not agree you should be forced to ignore your new existence. Therefore, if time permits, I would love to see you perform your ability. While in the privacy of our domus, I see no cause for you to refrain. I believe displaying it now will quell the desire, since you must not reveal it in public."

"Ah, yes," I say, fully understanding the bend of her words. I can't exactly fault her for this, especially since it's only temporary.

I lift my utensil to my mouth to avoid having to speak further. Her eyes are so bright with anticipation that I find it difficult to swallow. I force myself to keep eating, one slow bite after another. Hopefully, there will be no time left for me to show what may no longer exist. I will discover on my own. If I'm right, *then* I will confess.

I hear the apprehensive footsteps of my pater in the culina. He steps outside to join us. He brushes a hand through his thick, dark hair, his eyes shifting from me to my mater.

"Sapphire, do you think it wise for her to delight in a folly which we cannot condone? I will admit I was listening."

Heat rises to my face. I can't take this. "Mater, I have to leave. Otherwise I risk being tardy."

"Rayne, there is still plenty of time before Institute commences."

"The truth is, I have a headache," I say, avoiding my pater's gaze. "It may take me longer to walk in my current condition."

I stand up to leave, and she does something quite strange. She wraps her arms around me. It takes me a few seconds to remember the sensation. I feel myself caught in a dream. I allow her to hug me for as long as she wants then trot down the steps without looking back.

Soon I begin to run, dodging the trees and shrubbery in my path. I see an ancient stump of a once Great Pine several meters ahead. It's one of the few not yet restored.

I pass it each day on my route to Institute. Each lunar cycle brings hints of growth. When I was at Primary, I could leap onto it with ease. Now, I need a running start. It's come far these past ten years.

I run faster, calculating my stride. When a few meters separate me from it, I thrust my arms behind me and leap. I land squarely on top of it, planting my hands on its smooth surface to steady myself.

I intend to leap from it and continue my course to Institute, but I pause. It's almost like something beckons me to stay, to close my eyes and listen. It's as though it speaks to me, and I can hear its spirit.

I feel the energy coursing through my veins like they are the roots of this ancient stump. My fingers tingle. My palms pulse with a coolness contrary to the heat of my body. The longer my hands remain, the colder they become. I don't move them. I don't leave. I'm where I'm meant to be.

My body sways. My hands begin to sting from the cold …or poked, as if by a thousand pine needles. They grow numb from the sensation, and it invigorates me. I feel a gust of air blowing onto my face and into my nose. My balance feels unsteady, yet I don't fall.

I sense the life of the ancient stump stirring within me. I sway in the memories of its life. I heed the history of its roots and its branches boasting the majesty it once was. It speaks to me of its youth and its fruitful days.

It tells me of the day a weapon was wielded against it, snuffing its life for centuries. Now it wishes to sing. First, it must breathe.

With each wave of my breath, I sense its own growing stronger, faster, until it roars. I open my eyes as if stirring from a dream. I *can* open my eyes. I see the clouds above me, no longer shrouded by the canopy of trees.

My stomach leaps to my throat at what I see. The trunks no longer tower above me. They're below me. My eyes don't lie, but I know this can't be real. I must be dreaming.

I need to orient myself. My feet grip for stability on a surface which should be flat. Instead it's cylindrical and narrow and yielding to my weight.

My legs grow weak from fright. My feet slip. I feel myself falling. Needles scrape my flesh. My hands struggle to grip branches which shouldn't exist.

The moment I convince myself I'm still asleep in my pod, I feel the impact of the ground as I land on my back. My mind is confused. I close my eyes. I know when I open them, I'll find myself in my chamber.

The pain in my back and the scrapes on my flesh are real. What I feel isn't the soothing warmth of my floor. It's the soil of the Earth.

I open my eyes.

I focus on the tree towering above me. My mind has no explanation for what my eyes behold. It's a Pine, soaring to the clouds, its needles green with life.

There it stands, majestic and proud. There it stands in the place where the stump used to be.

I am now—somehow—a floresca, and the ability is mighty within me.

6

Mocking laughter awakens me. A male with pale-pink hair and a matching pointy beard hovers above me. I would consider him fair to behold if not for the deep scowl which usually contorts his face. He leans over the edge of his yellow-and-brown spotted zephyr-craft. It tilts enough for me to see his passenger. Her wide, green eyes are forced into a narrow squint.

I blink a few times, wondering why the light is different. I know where I am and what direction I face, yet the sun is on the opposite horizon of where it should be. I lift my hand to shield my eyes from the rays peeking through the canopy, and it hits me. I remember what happened.

I have flourished the Pine to its majesty of the past. This is too fantastical to be real. Soaring with the master eagle is somehow tangible in comparison. The tree is something entirely different.

I shiver at the fear of what or who I have become. I don't know why the Luminescence replaced my ability to whisper with another so powerful. I don't want to be a floresca. I want to fly.

Jhonis's sneering breath distracts me. With a single blink, animosity consumes me. I shift to my knees, wanting both of them to notice where we are, but they don't. Jhonis, at least, is too preoccupied with his taunts.

"Truly, Diamond, to miss a full day at Institute for sleep—*out here*—is so very appropriate. It would seem I was too generous earlier when I merely mocked her. Sape here truly is a beast of the wild."

"Then there is no point squandering words on her," Diamond yawns in the affectedly bored manner she does so well.

"Perhaps you have it right, Diamond. I wonder if she comprehends me any more than a pet canine of the Ancients."

I can't suppress a genuine smile. All he needs to do is turn his head to the left, and he'll see what I've done.

"Look, Diamond. The beast grins. If she had a tail, I do believe she would be wagging it." As he drags the phrasing of his words, I know he thinks he truly wounds me. "Oh, Diamond, do pardon me," he continues, his mouth drooping in a theatrical expression of regret. "How wrong of me to soil the goodness of a gentle beast of the wild. Canines have never caused me ill."

I have no desire to waste any energy on him. After everything that's happened, his words no longer have power over me. Soon, he and everyone will know what I did with the Pine—the *Great* Pine.

I curl my lips in a patronizing smile and say, "Jhonis, I wish for you to pilot your craft over the Great Canyon of the West and see where the winds will meet you." I turn to leave, but his words make me pause.

"You dare utter sentiments of physical assault against me, Sape? Not only do you behave as they do—I believe you *think* in the barbaric tongues!"

"And you are too inept to use any of them. A pity."

As I turn and run, Jhonis shouts something at me, but I pay no heed. I'm too busy laughing. He actually though what he said would bother me.

As the giraffe-patterned craft whooshes past me, Jhonis leans over the side and yells, "Vile Sape!"

I wave in response and yell back, "Catch you later!" I look to Diamond, expecting to see her face bunched in its usual display of disdain. Instead, she focuses her gaze on a point behind me. My stomach leaps to my throat. She's staring at the Great Pine.

I grin at her discovery until I realize something. She won't believe I did it, nor will anyone else. As I watch them disappear behind the trees, I stand in the presence of this fantastical thing, feeling sadness. The Luminescence has replaced my ability to fly with one I don't want.

I close my eyes and imagine I can still whisper. I imagine I can still summon the master eagle. I sigh and force the notion from my mind.

I wander to a Great Maple and mount its lowest branch. I rest my back against the trunk and prop my feet to steady myself. As I gaze up at the canopy, my chest becomes tight with sadness. If I were to climb, the master eagle would not hear my call.

Perhaps there is another way. He knows me. If he were to *see* me, would he come to me and offer me flight?

What if none before me ever flew on the back of greatness because they didn't think it was possible? Maybe it was never a matter of ability. Maybe I'm simply the first to try. I shake my head and reject the thought. Surely others have.

If I want to know, I just have to climb. Instead I remain with my back against the trunk, gazing at the bits of the early autumn sky, wishing I can fly.

"I'm losing my mind!" I scream in the ancient tongue.

It was all a dream. I'm still dreaming. I'm in my chamber, lying in my pod on my day of birth. None of this is real. I'm the same as I ever was.

My mind teeters on delirium as I hear my voice crackle. I feel my body tossing itself off the branch and landing on the ground with a thud.

"I have fallen onto my chamber floor, and still I sleep?" My voice shrieks with maniacal laughter at the vision of Jhonis returning and seeing me here like this.

"I *am* swine. No! I am a pet canine. I never awoke as susurrator nor as a floresca. I still lie sleeping in my pod, and I will prove it!" I shout to the trees and barely notice the creatures of the forest scurrying from my hysteria.

Lying on my back, I part my lips. In a haze of insanity, I imitate the inflection and feign the whisper of a susurrator. "Salvē, to the squirrels who scamper from my madness. Salvē, to the birds of all species who flitter in the trees. And you, Fox! I see you there with your conquest in your mouth. Come to me now. Delight with me, for I am a beast. *See?* I roll on my back like a pet canine."

I release another wave of hysterical laughter, but the rustling of leaves quiets me. Someone has come. I almost hope it's Jhonis. I blink to clear the tears from my eyes. I don't see his craft.

I shift onto my elbows and blink again as bushy tails, a flurry of wings, and a fox surround me. I force myself to my feet.

The sensation of panic courses through me, and I struggle to contain it. I close my eyes and focus on the rate of my breath. I try to calm it as I heed the sounds of nature: the song of the birds, the chatter of the squirrels, and the rustling of leaves. When I open them, they're all still here waiting for something.

They're waiting for me to whisper.

My shoulders rise and fall with my heaving breath. I don't know how this is possible, but it's real. I close my eyes and focus on the sounds of the forest, then I whisper words which they shouldn't understand.

"Salvē, creatures. I was wrong to summon you all. I bid you to return to your tasks before my interruption."

One after the other they all depart, flapping and scurrying and trotting into the trees. I expel the lingering panic through deep breaths, then I look to the sky, and I climb.

7

I awake this morning swimming in a sea of frenzy. I can whisper, and I can flourish. The concept both terrifies and thrills me.

I ready myself for the day, feeling like I'm floating. I don't stop to wonder what any of this means. Instead I remember the feeling of wind on my face and an eagle-eye view of the world.

I replay yesterday evening's events in my mind. When I reached the canopy of the Great Maple, I whispered to the sky, trusting the master eagle would hear me. He did. I remained up there with him until the last of the light was extinguished. Up there, I didn't care how I was still able to soar with him. I only reveled in the fact that I could.

Never before had I been absent for evening fare. My parentes were both worried, but I excused myself to my chamber before they could say much. I ignored my device when Rafe contacted me. I wanted to forget the concerns of the tangible world.

Now, in this bright, new day, all I want is to indulge in this feeling of happiness and ignore everything else.

When I enter the culina, no one is present. I hear no signs of my parentes. I step into the corridor and see light pouring in from their chamber. They always leave it open during the day. I pause to wonder why they've left earlier than normal but convince myself there's no cause for worry.

I grab an apple and pear from a vessel of fresh fruit. I take a bite from the pear when I hear footsteps in the corridor. They belong to my pater. My heart races as I realize I still don't want to see him. I make two quiet strides to the veranda threshold, deactivate it, and run down the steps. I think I'm ashamed of my behavior. I'm not ready to beg his forgiveness for my harsh words.

I clutch the fruit in my hand and run to the cover of trees. I lean against a trunk and devour both fruit, barely tasting their tangy juice.

I crouch to my knees, sink my hand into the soil and dig. When it's deep enough to cover the full length of my forearm, I place the core and pit into the hole and bury them.

I can't resist gazing at the bits of early morning sky peeking through the trees. I wish I could spend my days in flight, but I must tend to my life on the ground. I can't be absent from Institute three days in a row.

For the first time, I crave interaction with my age peers and the indifference of the magisters. They'll regard me as usual, but it won't have the same effect on me.

The deeper I stroll through the forest, the more I succumb to a daze of possibilities. I pause when I hear the humming of voices in the distance. As I search for the source, the volume increases. Seven are gathered at the spot which used to be an ancient stump.

I conceal myself behind a Spruce. As I press my lips to quiet the sound of my breath, I inhale the herbal scent of the old tree. I lift a hand to part the branches. I have an obscured view of the group, but I know them all. All of them are florescae. In the midst of the natural colors of hair, I see the unmistakable dark, shiny tresses of my mater.

I can't hear their words, and I struggle to discern the intonation of their voices. As I watch my mater between the narrow field of the branches, one of the florescae turns toward me. I slowly remove my hand from the branch and crouch.

This is pointless. I can't hear anything, and if I reveal myself now, they'll know I was listening.

A grouping of Spruce and Firs are to my left. I take a series of cautious steps, making a wide arc around the seven florescae. When my passage is clear, I shake my arms to release the bits of tension.

I turn to correct my course toward Institute and notice the wolf pack of my colony. I watch the pup and the alpha female, losing myself in the beauty of their nature. The pup paws at her, and she turns to nudge him forward. I smile at their familial bond of affection.

As I watch them, I find myself—for the second time in my life—wondering about the source of my birth. It's strange to think of it now, yet I can't ignore it. The first time I wondered about it, I was two, so young that it was only fleeting.

Something occurs to me. It's so logical that I wonder why it didn't until now. The answers I seek—the explanation of what's happening to me—must lie in my DNA.

I force my feet forward, my mind a swirl of thoughts I can't contain. If I'm to confirm this, I have to ask my parentes. The idea is daunting. I've never discussed the details of my birth with them. I don't know how to begin such a conversation.

Another idea occurs to me. My parentes reacted as though I was the first, but maybe there are others like me. The Board possesses birth knowledge of all citizens. If anyone knows why this is happening to me, it'll be them.

Members of the Board will come to our domus—as they would have done the morn of my second year. All I have to do is ask one of them.

I release an exuberant sigh. When I reach the edge of the forest, I realize how engrossed I've been in my thoughts. I've already arrived at Institute.

The geometric structure lies 100 meters from me. Its main triangular section of glass and titanium stands like a prism of splendor amidst a sea of forest.

Now that I'm here, I'm too excited to discuss anything. But until the Board comes, I have to act like nothing has changed. My mater will be happy to hear it.

I step onto a square grid of quartz and onyx. The rays of the sun reflect on the surface, causing a brilliant, shimmering effect. Whenever I cross it, I feel as though I walk upon stars.

I squint from the glare and tap my fingers. My holodigit activates, I make two circular motions with my index finger, and a dark, translucent band appears in front of my eyes.

Subordinate citizens zoom past me en route to the zephyr station on the north end of the Plaza. Several younger citizens ride their zephyr-boards toward the main entrance. They all hop to the ground to dismount, eager for their day of knowledge.

Amidst the swirl of colorfully dyed hair is the black, flowing robes of the magisters. As they stroll among us, none seem concerned with the action surrounding them.

A sculpture twice my height sits on the southwest end of the plaza. Rafe is the artist. It's a slender, rugged piece composed of iron and glass. To me it resembles a bonsai of the

Ancients, with glass where there should be needles.

I settle my eyes on it, realizing I'm not sure where I'm supposed to be. Discussions convene either on the grounds, in the main structure, or the Annex. As I watch the scene, it occurs to me I have to think about what day this is. My cheeks puff from a stifled laugh, and I shake my head.

I begin with two days prior, the day of my birth. It was *dies Gandhi*. One day prior was *dies Da Vinci*. Therefore, this is *dies Mandela*. Now I know where I must go.

My first discussion is at the Annex to the south of the main structure. It's a 400-meter circular path of 10 meters wide and hovers 40 meters above ground. It's modeled after the ancient times when such a surface was used for sporting events during the warmer months. I still can't comprehend a spectrum of capability that would make competition of sport possible.

The only way to access the Annex is to climb the rope or ladders of steel which are bolted to the structure. Subordinate citizens at Secondary use the ropes. The magisters and children at Primary use the steel.

I select the closest rope which hasn't filled to capacity. When I'm a few paces from it I run, throw my arms in front of me and leap onto it. I place one hand above the other and hoist my feet to climb to the surface. Two of my age peers are still above me when I near the top, so I slow my ascent.

It doesn't take me long to reach the surface. I swing my

legs and toss them over the edge. I land in a crouched position, my fingers sinking into the rough and spongy synthetic material.

Five groups of ten are gathering at their usual meeting points. My group on *Mammals of Extinction* assembles at our customary location at the southwest bend. The Annex is my favorite location for discussion. Up here I have an unhindered view of the majestic Great Mountains.

Our magister coughs to gain our attention, so my time for gazing is ended. He strolls backward as he guides us around the path. All magisters lead discussion in this manner to emulate Aristotle.

Though it's my first day at Institute after missing two days, none will react as though they've noticed. We must only focus on the magister and concepts related to our discussion.

We walk around the surface at a pace to match the others so no group gets too close to another. When the discussion begins, I find it nearly impossible to engage.

From this angle I have a clear view of the Tank. I can detect the shimmering surface of water as the rays of the sun reflect onto it. As we continue our stroll, my eyes linger. Suddenly, I wish to swim.

The Tank is my treasured place to do so. People from nearby colonies in this province of Coloratus go there to swim and dive. It's a colossal vessel of concrete and steel. Even from this distance I can see the head of a white horse which adorns the exterior wall, a relic of the Ancients. The undulating form of the upper rim makes it all the more beautiful to behold.

I realize how much of the discussion I haven't heard when I notice a female named Sphinx rapidly moving her lips. It's time for me to engage.

"You miss the bend of my statement, Magister Lucius. By stating the magnificence of the dolphin and the whale, I do not mean to deflect from the majesty of extinct creatures of land. The elephant, the polar bear, the Bengal tiger, and countless others of the large mammals were most glorious. I do not deny this. I merely mean to say I, in a matter of pure opinion, feel the Earth suffers the greatest loss from the extinction of its mammals of the oceans."

When Sphinx says nothing more, a male named Akane speaks next. "The sentiments of Sphinx should be of no surprise, Magister Lucius. She is an aquamarist, after all. In her eyes, no creature is as grand as those who once inhabited the seas and oceans."

"Yes, Magister Lucius," Sphinx continues, "Perhaps you fail to appreciate my perspective via this elemental basis."

"Citizen Sphinx, I do not mean to suggest you are unfound in your ardor. My retort only meant to suggest this. We would be remiss if we did not hold in esteem *all* noble creatures—both land and sea—who have no descendants such that we might still behold their majesty. We must be prudent to revere them all. Each of these mammals warrants this and more."

A shadow moves above us, distracting me from the conversation. A hawk flies over the summit of the main structure toward the forest. She lowers her flight to the canopy. With a graceful swoop of her wings, she dives into the leaves, then soars to the east, clutching a snake in her talons. I lift my hand to shield my eyes from the sun as I watch her fade in the distance. All I can think of now is how much I long for flight.

The sound of faint snickering distracts me. I force my eyes from the sky and realize it's directed at me.

Everyone in our group is facing me. The magister folds his arms, his lips tightly pressed, his eyes filled with admonishment. I can't decide whether it's against me or the snickering.

The magister must have asked me a question. I'm too embarrassed to ask him to repeat it. Then I realize something. None of them are looking directly at me. They're looking at something behind me.

I spin around, and irritation replaces my confusion. It's Jhonis. Why he's here, I don't know. His discussion group on *Astrophysics in The Rebirth Period* convenes on the opposite end of the Annex. I turn in search of his group to confirm. I see them there, still following their magister in her stroll.

The other groups behind us are beginning to slow their approach. Jhonis is causing a spectacle, and soon everyone will be focused on us.

I return my attention to him. There he stands, gazing at

the sky with a feigned expression of bewilderment. The snickering grows louder when he strokes his fingers through imaginary locks of hair, his mouth slackening, his eyes drooping.

My face flushes from at his mockery of me. I don't care who sees it. I open my mouth in rebuke, but remind myself that my anger is what he craves. He has no power over me. No longer am I a person of inferiority. I remember who I've become.

All on the Annex have stopped to witness this farce. They all know I'm the object of his ridicule. No one speaks. They all anticipate my response. I have no desire to placate them.

I turn to leave without formally excusing myself with the magister. There's no need. He merely observes as the other magisters do, offering no words of rebuke to Jhonis for disrupting first discussion.

I take a few steps toward a rope when I hear the voice which I singularly despise.

"To where do you depart, *Sape?* Do you return to the forest floor such as I have witnessed you, rolling in the soil like the wild beast you are?"

The snickering increases in volume. I can't believe their audacity to break from propriety. With each voice cracking in suppressed laughter, they encourage Jhonis to continue his taunt. To them I'm no one. The rules of decorum don't apply to me.

I can no longer tolerate this scene, yet leaving will only

empower him. I must end it now.

"All of you who stand before me now, heed my words. By your uncivilized encouragement of this provocation, each one of you makes me wonder if I have reversed in time. Is this the age of that despicable term, bullying? Or do we now live in The Rebirth Period? I wonder," I seethe, forcing my shaking fingers to tap in calculated contemplation against my chin.

"It would seem Sape has learned to imitate proper speech. It reminds me of the primates who learned the language of hands to communicate with the Ancients. Except, those creatures were more intelligent than she."

The snickering teeters on genuine laughter. They don't care about codes of conduct where I'm concerned. I'm beneath them. I'm nothing.

Yet, I'm not. I'm more powerful than any of them.

No.

I refuse to succumb to self-boasting. I have to calm myself. It's best to ignore them.

I channel my anger into a mental form so I can control it. I condense the sensation until it becomes a ball which hovers within my grasp. I close my eyes and focus on it, ignoring everyone around me.

I see it clearly: a gray ball of wispy cotton. The airy orb draws closer to me, and I inject my negative energy into it. The voices quiet as the orb grows larger. It's no longer a ball. It expands into an undefined shape while maintaining its cottony essence. It shifts to a deep gray as dark as cinders.

Suddenly, I feel cold. Uncommonly cold. I ignore it as I wrap myself in tranquility.

The orb rises above me, and I feel like I'm floating. My eyes moisten in the serenity of it all. Tears flow to my cheeks. They dance on the edges of my vision like tiny currents of lightning. My tears float above me, drifting to the sky and absorbing into the atmosphere. Now they are falling, but I don't feel them. They go elsewhere.

Whispering voices and anxious gasps distract me. I open my eyes, the rains cease, and the orb and the tears have vanished. The first person I see is Jhonis. His pale-pink hair is saturated with water. His garments are drenched. His body writhes, and his eyes are wide with fear. Everyone else is dry.

"What abomination is this?" he shrieks. "How does rain fall from the sky and seek only *me?* This is no work of an aerisma. It was *you*." He faces me, his wide mouth retracting into a sneer. "What dark magic of the Sapes did you wield?"

I open my mouth to answer, but I can think of no words. I can't think at all as I stare at the sea of frightened faces. Yet, none of them regards me with accusation. Of course they don't think I did this. No one could have done this.

None can call forth rain. What just happened is no matter of heightened ability. This is new, and I don't know what to call it. I only know the Luminescence must have gifted it to me.

Sturdy hands clutch my arms. They belong to Jhonis. A wave of ferocity seizes me. His eyes, narrowed in spite, pierce my own. Suddenly I want to strike him.

"You dare lay your hands on me, *Jhonis?*"

"Why should I not? Your inane existence is beneath any level of respect."

I survey the crowd. None show disdain for this heinous physical act. I've had enough. My eyes narrow, and my lips curl into a mocking smile.

"You have it wrong. It is you who is beneath me. Regard yourself, Jhonis. *You* place your hands on *me*. You prove yourself to be boorish and lacking all decency. You forsake all sense of self-control. I refuse to be the object of your barbarism. Remove your hands from me."

"You dare rebuke me, Sape? It is I who—"

"Away with you, Jhonis!" I feel the heat of rage, but I force my voice to remain steady. I no longer care about all those in our midst. I only care to be free from his taunts forever. "Look around you. See the spectacle you cause. You have disrupted the course of all these discussions."

"It was whatever dark magic hungers for your tainted soul which—"

"May the storm of whatever magic you proclaim it to be follow you always. As for this day and all the rest, I am done with your insults. I am done with your contempt. I am done with *you*. Speak to me no further. Show your face to me no further. Taunt me no further, or you will find the sum of your dreams and desires lies in the deepest depths of what the Ancients called *Hell*."

My chest heaves. My heart pounds. I turn from him and seek the eyes of any who dare meet my own. No one speaks, not even him. Yet, his eyes shout. They declare his hatred and betray his plotting thoughts.

I turn my back on him and on them all and make a few running strides to the edge of the Annex. I crouch to my knees and fling myself over the edge. My hands grip the rope, and I propel myself to the ground. I don't look up to see if they watch me. I don't listen to the words Jhonis shouts at me. I reach the ground, and I don't stop. Once again I'm running but not from them. I'm running towards my new reality.

8

My head is spinning. *I* am spinning. I comb my hands through my hair and pull, as if the act will erase my confusion.

Three.

I possess three abilities, the last of which is something entirely unprecedented. I should feel anxious and alone, but I don't. Up there on the Annex, something changed for me. I can't explain it. I only know I'm content. Maybe it's just adrenaline convincing me of this.

I don't know where I'll go. I only know I don't want to be alone.

Rafe.

There are two hours remaining until our midday fare.

Though it's fleeting, my heart sinks at the possibility that he won't come. I already missed two of our rendezvous. He may choose to abandon a third.

I fiddle with my holodigit. He's probably working, and I don't want to disturb him. I decide to go early and wait for him. If he doesn't come, then I'll contact him. I just want our comradeship to be restored. I hope he does too.

I have many kilometers to travel before I reach our spot. It's too great a distance to go on foot. I decide to use my favorite means of travel for long distance. I must locate a horse. I hope it will be my favorite, the black stallion, the only one I've ever seen anywhere near my colony. I usually find him in the quiet of the forest perimeter, though sometimes he ventures into the Colony Plaza.

He's never allowed anyone to mount him except me. No susurrator has ever compelled him, and it's immoral to force the will of a creature. In my 14th year, a herd of horses were gathered at a stream. Jhonis and Diamond were present. I remember approaching the horses, struggling to ignore their jeers. As I prepared to mount the closest horse, Jhonis wrongfully displayed his ability. He summoned them all from me except one: the black stallion.

I'll never forget the sound of his mocking laugh as he said, "There, Sape. I have left one to you. Mount him if you can."

I can almost hear their pretentious laughter. That day I refused to sulk in defeat. I approached the black stallion at the stream, knowing my attempt would be futile. I stood there, gazing into his eyes, him meeting mine with no indication of his intent to flee.

I recall him lowering his head and planting his hooves, resolved to remain in his spot. He was acknowledging me as a rider. It was enough to convince me to act. Without pause, I took a few trotting steps and leapt. I grabbed his satiny mane into my fists as I swung my leg over the tail end of his back.

I remember what it was like when he neighed, imploring me to lead him. I nudged him toward my path, forgetting Jhonis and Diamond were there. As I rode past them though, I reveled in their bitter grimaces.

As my feet lead me southward, I wonder if he'll sense I've changed. I've always suspected the reason he permitted me travel was he didn't sense the Luminescence within me. If it's true, he'll likely refuse me now.

After a kilometer, I see him standing, graceful and proud, in a clonal colony of infant Aspens. As he dips his head to drink from a stream, his shiny coat radiates against the white bark of the trees.

I approach him as I always do, respectful of his grace. When I'm several paces from him, my stride becomes a trot. Ignoring the thought that he'll flee, I leap. I fling my leg over his back as my hands find their familiar grasp in his mane.

I lean forward and inhale the scent of him and feel the tenseness of his muscles. He stomps the ground more assertively than he ever has with me. When he lifts his head and neighs, I know he must sense the abilities within me. I drape my arms around him and rub his flank to reassure him.

"It has been too long, Black Stallion, has it not?"

He neighs and stomps the ground again, but less forcefully so. I continue speaking to him as I normally would, knowing he will not understand my words. "Fancy a ride to the Tower? It is much too far for me to make the journey on foot, Black Stallion. I would be indebted to you."

I sense he is unsure of me still, so I don't urge him. Instead I rub his flank and press my ear to his back to study the rate of his breath. I wait for him to decide whether he wishes to oblige or to buck. I do nothing. I say nothing. What happens next is for him to decide.

His breathing calms, his legs stand firm. He lowers his head, and I know he's made his choice.

He prances and neighs, beckoning me to direct him, so I do. I tug gently on his mane and nudge him with my legs and feet. He rides swifter, and my eyes water with the familiar breeze of riding horseback. A sudden impulse urges me to search the skies, but I don't dare. I won't dishonor the pride of the black stallion for want of the master eagle. Instead I relish this moment.

When we arrive at the forest perimeter, I tap my fingers to activate my device. I still have well beyond an hour before midday fare. I decide to walk the remaining distance on foot. I swing my leg over his back and leap to the ground. He nudges me, and I stroke his face.

"Thank you, Black Stallion. I hope to see you again soon." He blinks his brown eyes and whinnies. I offer a few final pats. He turns from me in a trot, disappearing into the cover of trees.

I turn toward the plains of wild grass and see the Tower two kilometers to the east. All are welcome to enter as they please. Rafe and I do so each midday.

It's nearly 100 meters in height and is composed of concrete, iron, and steel. The bombings of the Homo sapiens destroyed it. Now it's a relic, restored at the dawn of The Rebirth Period.

They sent bombs into the skies to destroy one another. Generations ago, Homo praestans took measures to ensure the survival of our own species, first operating in secret until our numbers outranked their own. Now the Tower serves no purpose beyond a reminder of where humankind has been.

We have no need to monitor the skies. Our zephyrs can't travel at such heights, and our interest in astronomy lies only in the preservation of Earth.

I find myself considering these notions as I approach the Tower. I'm anxious to see Rafe. I'm not sure what I will say to him. I do know I need to assure him I no longer feel betrayed by his alignment with my pater. Of course he reacted the way he did. I can't fault him for it.

The prairie grass transitions to a field of wildflowers of purples, yellows, and reds. I navigate a narrow path of mulch and earthen pebbles, which leads directly to the Tower.

When I'm half a kilometer away, I see movement through the window thresholds in the uppermost region. A silver fabric covers them to prevent birds from nesting inside the Tower. One of the sheets is pulled to the side. Someone is in there. Rarely does anyone come here, so I think it's Rafe.

The person waves to me. It *is* him. I wish I could fly to reach him faster. As my long strides become a run, I can't wait to confide in him.

When I reach the base of the Tower, I enter a quadratic space of concrete walls. It smells of emptiness and dust. I step deeper into the space, following a ray of natural light spilling through the entry. A blue light is illuminated behind a transparent, cylindrical wall to my right. It's the ascensus, the only means of reaching the summit.

I wave my hand in front of the blue light, and the barrier dissolves. I cross the threshold and count to three. The barrier seals, I hold my breath, and I become weightless for the ten-second ascent to the top.

A green light indicates the restoration of oxygen, and I breathe the tepid air. My legs fall smoothly to the ground, and before the barrier dissolves, I see Rafe. His smile is wide and inviting, but there's a hint of something else in his eyes: concern.

"Rayne, you will never know how pleased I am you have come. I do believe this third time was the charm."

I cross the threshold, unable to contain my grin. "You have no idea how glad I am to see you. I feared you would abandon our ritual."

"Never."

He offers his hand, and I accept it. He pulls me toward him, and I wrap myself in the familiarity of his embrace. I almost don't notice the stark, pale surroundings as he leads me to our spot.

The uppermost room of the Tower is a pentagonal space of concrete. The middle portion is open to the elements, save for the sheets of shimmering, silver fabric.

"You are early." It's the only thing I can think to say.

"So are you," he says as he holds one of the sheets aside for me. "I have just come from the Harvesting Center."

He picks up a basket of woven bark, and I feel guilty. For two days he brought sustenance for us, and I didn't bother to come. I peer into the basket, my mouth salivating at the first thing I see: thinly sliced, deliciously fresh boar hind.

"I must say, I found myself in a state of anticipation. Would you come, or would I again dine alone on all this?" Though he smiles, his eyes betray the truth. He means what he says.

I offer what I hope is a reassuring smile as I climb through the opening. At this height, the wind is fierce. I lean forward to steady myself before grabbing the metal ladder. I place my foot on the lowest rung and climb.

I reach the top and crouch to protect myself from the force of the wind. I crawl to a cylindrical dome in the center of the roof and lean against it to shield myself. I breathe the brisk wind and savor the height. Up here I can see everything.

To the west lies the Great Mountains. To the east of the range is the vast forest. At this height, there's only the sparsest hint of human presence. I can neither see our Institute nor the Tank. What I can see is the only track of our hovertram system which sits above the canopy of trees. It terminates at the foothills of the mountains. It's barely visible from here, but I can still detect its steel structure.

I turn to the north and south, and all I see are the lightning and wind farms which extend for kilometers. Beyond them are the distant colonies of the plains and other provinces of this realm.

I hear Rafe ascending the ladder. His blood-orange hair blows in the wind against the tapestry of wildflowers. It's a beautiful sight.

He tosses the basket over the ledge, and I catch it. He climbs onto the surface and settles next to me. As we huddle against the dome, I fiddle with the handles. Again I'm unsure what to say. The concept is odd to me. I don't know why I find myself nervous in his presence lately. I can only attribute it to my secret.

He shifts closer to me and leans his head against mine. "Worry not, Rayne. I am not jealous of the master eagle. It was an adventure for you."

His words soothe me. He turns to whisper into my ear as if the wind is too loud for me to hear his words. "I understand your cause for being absent these two days prior. I know you believe I betrayed you in my seeming alliance with your pater. I never meant for you to feel as such."

I want to tell him the reason I didn't come yesterday, that I slipped into a state of unconsciousness after flourishing the ancient stump. I can't find the right words, so instead I say, "You are blameless. What I regret is my own behavior."

He wraps his arm around me, and I nuzzle closer. I relax in the sensation of his warmth on my left and the briskness of the wind on my right. It's a familiar sensation which I've missed.

This is my moment to confide, yet something within me prevents it. I don't know how he'll react. I stare into his tawny-brown eyes, losing myself in their warmth. Then I choose to say something else that's true. "I hope you understand my position. I find myself slow to adjust to my new…existence."

"Rayne." He sighs my name with a throaty lure, and I nestle further onto his chest. "While I cannot fathom your situation, please know I understand why you have been distant. What has happened to you must be beyond difficult for you to bear. Mirificus, yes, but difficult still."

"Thank you for understanding. You have no idea what it means to me."

He gazes at me for a moment, then winks and says, "Would you mind handing me the basket? Suddenly I find myself famished."

I lift it from my lap and swing it around so it catches him on the chest.

"Careful. My heart has not yet fully healed from the wound of your absence." Though he laughs and grabs his chest in play, the way he looks at me, I almost believe him.

"I am in no mood to be mocked."

He grabs a pomegranate and two hard-boiled duck eggs from the basket. "Perhaps a bit of folly to lighten our spirits."

He tosses the eggs into the air and juggles. After a few turns, he pitches one of them to me, playfully out of reach. In pure reflex, I grab his wrist for balance and extend my free hand. I catch the egg in my palm before it plummets 100 meters to the ground.

He feigns to ignore me as he searches the basket. He removes a slice of kiwi and holds one to my lips, smiling at me expectantly. "In the chance of you dropping the egg."

I toss my head back and laugh. I grab the kiwi from his hand and pop it into my mouth. He slips his arm around me as he stuffs bites of cured meat into his own.

Up here, everything that happened since my day of birth seems manageable. As I gaze across the horizon, enjoying the view, I feel better than I ever have.

9

I wander the rooms of my villa, wondering where my parentes could be. It's past the hour of evening fare. They should've returned by now.

After my time with Rafe, I had no desire to complete my day at Institute. I came here, knowing I couldn't avoid my parentes indefinitely. Now it's them who avoid me.

The growling in my stomach convinces me not to wait for them. I enter the culina and browse in the cold storage. On the center shelf is a ceramic container with something written on the lid:

Enjoy your evening fare, Rayne. We will return prior to the 19th hour.

My hands shake with guilt. I've shown them discourtesy for too long. They no longer wish to tolerate it. They mean for me to dine alone.

My mouth waters at the contents of the dish: roasted pheasant topped with my favorite mushroom and sherry sauce; sautéed asparagus, and fresh tomatoes. I'm so hungry, I don't bother warming it. It doesn't take me long to finish. Now there's nothing to do but wait.

I meander the corridor, swinging around the trunks of Aspens. If I go to my chamber, I know my parentes will leave me to myself. I decide to await their return in the salon. It's an open space with only one containing wall, a mixture of bright starkness and earthy comfort.

Adjacent to the single wall are two lounges covered in refurbished leather and buffalo hide. In the center of the room is a long, low table of concrete. It's encased in the same coating as the walls, making it smooth to the touch.

Strips of lighting illuminate from the ceiling. I sink onto one of the lounges and prop my feet on the table. I decide to entertain myself while I wait. I activate my holodigit and say, "Transmit *The Cosmos Chronicles, Set 4*."

A glowing field appears, and the transmission begins. It doesn't play long when I hear footsteps in the culina. My heart beats rapidly, and a nervous chill flows through me. My parentes have returned.

I stop the transmission and compose myself. As I wait for

them to discover I'm here, I struggle to find the words I will say. I realize I only hear one set of footsteps in the corridor. They belong to my pater. Now I'm even more anxious.

"Rayne?"

"Yes, Pater. I am in the salon."

He steps around one of the Aspens and stops at the edge of the room. He looks as nervous as I feel.

"I am pleased you are here, Rayne." His voice cracks as he speaks, and the bitterness I've felt for him crumbles. He doesn't want a confrontation any more than I do.

"I returned just after midday. I did not feel fit enough to return to Institute."

He fiddles with his fingers and raises his eyebrows in wonder. "I see. Well. Do pardon the absence of your mater and myself. Your mater believed you might do well with some time to yourself. She thought it prudent for you to decide when you were ready to be amongst us."

"Oh," I say, relieved. "Pater…thank you. Perhaps Mater was right. I feel like myself again."

"I am pleased to hear it." He clears his throat and stares at me as if he expects me to say something else. Then I remember. I owe him an apology.

"Pater, I hope you will pardon my insolence when last we spoke. I should not have said those things. Please forgive me."

He fiddles with the soft fabric of his bottoms, taking a few timid steps into the salon. "Of course I forgive you. Please know I never intended to insult you. I simply lack the verbal prowess which comes to you and your mater so easily. Please also know my opinions are now fully in line with hers."

"They are?"

He nods and cracks a nervous smile. His eyes shift from my face to a point just beyond me. He's unsure of himself in my presence, and my heart melts because of it.

"Per viam, where is Mater?"

"Oh! She is partaking in yoga at the Overpass Gardens. She should return shortly."

Whenever their duties permit, my mater and the other florescae assemble on the Overpass Gardens for yoga. It's an expanse of gardens atop concrete columns. It extends for many kilometers. There are several, some of which expand to other provinces.

"Then neither of you have consumed evening fare?"

"No. I mean to say yes, we did. We dined with Sirs Aeron and Pettis."

"I hope the day finds them well."

"It does. I offered pardons for your absence."

"Thank you, Pater."

His eyes dart around the room again as he says, "I will retire to my chamber now."

"Pater, would you like to view a transmission with me? That is if you do not find yourself too fatigued."

His eyes dance about the room. I think I've surprised him.

"If you would have my company, I would rather enjoy it."

He walks across the floor and sits on the opposite end of the second lounge. He's as far from me as he can be in this space. As he poses himself stiffly on the lounge, I remind myself he's still here, and I credit him for it.

"What would you like to view, Pater?"

"What would I? I suppose...I will defer to you. I will be content with whatever you wish."

"How about *The Cosmos Chronicles?*"

"Mirificus," he says with a single, genuine clap of approval. "Which set?"

"Four."

"Ah yes, it is a compelling one. I will be delighted to view it again. Allow me to do the honors—except..." He lifts his right hand, realizing he's not wearing his holodigit.

"There, Pater," I say, pointing at the table.

"Ah! Thank you. I nearly forgot where last I placed it." He leans forward to retrieve it. "Very well. Now, allow me to..." He fumbles with placing the device on his fingers. I've always found it humorous that a sciens like him has trouble using the very technology he develops. He still uses the old holopad for his duty. He says the holodigit is a device meant for subordinate citizens. "If you do not mind, Rayne, perhaps you should initiate the transmission. I believe it would be more efficient."

"Very well, Pater."

Before I tap my fingers, the com sounds. We have a visitor. I point my index finger at it, and Rafe's image appears. I glance at my pater. His jaws are now clenched and his lips are tightened in irritation. His reaction tells me that everything's back to normal.

"It would appear our viewing is delayed."

I run to the entry and press my palm to the panel to deactivate the barrier. "Rafe! What a surprise. Come in."

"To what should we attribute your visit, Rafe?" my pater asks, not bothering to hide his annoyance. "Surely there must be some pressing matter. You come unannounced at such a disagreeable time."

"Pater, it is a perfectly agreeable hour."

"Do pardon me, Sir Roman. It appears you have forgotten my cause for coming." Rafe offers my pater a knowing tilt of the head, but my pater only frowns.

"I am ignorant of what you refer, I assure you."

"Sir Roman."

Confused by the exchange, I grab Rafe's hand and lead him into the salon. "Why *are* you here, Rafe? What is it you think my pater should know?"

"I have come to—ah, good eve, Lady Sapphire."

I turn to see my mater standing in the corridor, dressed in a lilac body suit. She enters with a warm smile as if nothing between us has changed.

"Good eve. I heard your voices in the culina."

"How was yoga?" I ask.

"Delightful. Did you discover the fare I prepared for you?"

"Yes. It was delicious."

She smiles and says, "Roman, I do hope you have offered our guest drink."

My pater twitches at his sudden inclusion. "Rafe has only just arrived."

"Thank you, Lady Sapphire, but I assure you, I do not require it. I have come as scheduled, though Sir Roman seems to have forgotten why."

"Roman, perhaps you should reflect upon four days prior," my mater says with a wink.

My pater bunches his lips as his eyes spark with understanding. Yet, he says nothing. I can't tolerate this anymore.

"Now that the three of you are in accord, why am I the sole person to remain in ignorance? Rafe, tell me now. What is the cause for your arrival? Do not hold me in suspense."

"Roman," my mater says before Rafe can respond. "Will you not assist me in preparing my bath?"

"Is the drainage malfunctioning? Do you require my assistance to repair it?"

My mater shakes her head and sighs. "Come away now, Roman. Allow these two a moment of privacy. You need not stand as sentry."

My pater follows her to their chamber, and I'm alone with Rafe. When he offers a mischievous smile, I become even more impatient.

"Tell me what this is about right now, or I will be quite cross with you."

"You will love it. It has everything to do with a gift for your day of birth. I hope you did not think I forgot to get you something this year."

"A gift! I forgot myself."

"Then trust me when I say all the better. You see, I have acquired two passes this night to attend the musical performance of—"

"The Daughters of Lennon!" I scream, my excitement suppressing any display of good manners.

"Of course," he laughs, taking my hands in his. "The moment I learned their performance was so near to your day of birth, I knew it was the perfect gift."

"This is mirificus, Rafe. Mater! Pater!" I find myself running into the corridor.

I hear the light footsteps of my mater and the clunking steps of my pater behind her. I run to her and wrap my arms around her.

"You have known of this since *dies Teresa?*"

"Yes, we have," she laughs.

"I am permitted to attend?"

"Of course. We would not refuse you such a thing. Besides, you are nearly of age. Do I not speak truth, Roman?"

"To renege would be uncivil."

"If you do not mind, Lady Sapphire and Sir Roman, the

hour is upon us. We must be off at once. I assure you both I will restore Rayne to you at a decent hour. I give you my word of honor, we will not delay."

"We know you will give us no cause for worry. As for you, Rayne, your pater and I wish for you to experience a musical night of youthful mirth."

"Thank you, all of you." As I pull Rafe toward the entry of guests I add with a grin, "A night of sound rest to you both. Do not force yourselves to stand vigil. Set yourselves to your pod at your usual hour. As for myself, I will see you in the morn."

10

We're several meters from the tram terminal when I begin skipping toward it. I don't care who sees me. The tram system is powered by electromagnetic energy. Their course extends for kilometers, weaving its web throughout the province.

The terminal sits several meters above ground and is accessed by an ascensus. Many of our age peers are already waiting for it. No children, their parentes, or elders are present. On this night, they leave us to ourselves.

When the ascensus is empty, Rafe and I cross the threshold for the quick ascent to the platform. As we await the tram, I observe the crowd. Some of them are looking at me. I know at least one of them was on the Annex this morn. I turn from them all and focus on Rafe.

He must notice, because he slips his arm around me.

"Once we arrive at the performance, we will be afforded plenty of space to avoid them all. As for now, try to ignore them."

A breeze whips through the structure, and I begin to shiver. Rafe pulls me closer until the musical chimes of Beethoven signal the tram's arrival.

"A night of bliss awaits," Rafe says.

It stops at the platform and the barriers retract. I grab his hand to pull him inside and immediately go to my favorite spot.

The front end is encased in glass, giving a panoramic view of the landscape. The barriers close, and we exit the terminal with a smooth glide.

The tram climbs to its long-distance height above the tree line. The world outside is mysterious and dazzling in the darkness of night. I imagine we're travelling through space. At this great speed, I feel wild and free.

Voices creep into my consciousness. When I repeatedly hear the word, pine, I'm coaxed into listening.

"The florescae are ignorant of the cause of this phenomenon?" a female voice asks.

"Affirmative. Inquisitors from the Capitolium arrived several hours prior," another female voice answers.

A male voice speaks next. "How is it none can ascertain at what point the ancient stump was flourished? To have seemingly sprouted in the course of a day—how can such a thing be? Surely, the florescae must simply have erred in their account of it. By nature they are an abstracted sort."

"It is not only they who attest to it. It is the route of Diamond and Jhonis to Institute. Diamond confirms it. In the morn it was a stump. Upon their return, it was a Great Pine," the first female voice explains.

"Why do we not inquire of Donatella? Her mater is a floresca. Where is she?" the male asks.

"Why do we not ask Ray—Ouch! That *hurt.*"

When the trio lower their voices to a whisper, I try to ignore them by focusing on the scene beyond the glass. Rafe wraps his arm around my shoulders and offers a warm squeeze. "Just a while longer."

Then I hear a voice laced with spite. It belongs to one of Jhonis's comrades. His name is Grindol. His thick brows the color of lime form a menacing arch on his face. His matching lime hair rests limply on his shoulders. He stands near the trio and speaks loudly so all in the tram can hear. "What do you know of this, Sape? I heard you were napping adjacent to it like a beast, so surely you must have some words to speak on it."

Rafe wraps his arms tighter around me and whispers, "I beg of you to allow me the joy of a retort." I shake my head.

The tram falls silent as everyone awaits my response. I scan the crowd and notice Diamond on the opposite end. Her green-streaked hair covers her face so I can't see her expression. Jhonis stands beside her, studying the nails of his fingers with an exaggerated display of intrigue.

"Diamond was present. I suggest you seek her opinion on the matter."

"Her mater is not a floresca such as Lady Sapphire. You know, your mater *adoptive.*"

"My mater has not yet had the opportunity to inform me of their discoveries. I assure you, once I do learn of their theory, you will be the last person with whom I share it."

I breathe deeply to calm my quivering shoulders. Rafe offers me a reassuring squeeze but remains silent. I feel the muscles of his chest flexing. I don't look at him, but as Grindol offers no rebuttal, I know Rafe is defending me without words.

Grindol sneers then squeezes through the crowd. He joins Jhonis who normally would have led the taunt. I'm glad he remembers my threat. He whispers to Diamond, and she reacts with a frown and bunching of her fuchsia-painted lips.

No one else speaks to me. Grindol and most others in the tram turn to Jhonis, expecting him to engage. Instead he remains silent. The confrontation has ended.

A gentle murmur of voices soon crescendos to a spirited volume. I expel my breath in a relieved sigh. Now I can relax. I focus on our destination and my earlier excitement. When I see the majestic form of the rosy sedimentary rocks, I feel my mouth forming a wide smile, and all the triviality is forgotten.

The tram slows in its approach of the terminal. It carries

us above one of two massive rocks which form the borders of the amphitheater. Between the two rock pillars is a great expanse of moss-covered seating and stone steps. At the base of it all is the performance platform, spotlighted by an outcrop of sedimentary rock behind it. I press my nose to the glass and gaze upon the splendor below us. From this height, the view is breathtaking.

Hundreds from colonies around the province already gather in the amphitheater, and dozens of others descend the tram terminals. Our tram stops, everyone disembarks, yet I linger. I watch the crowd gathering below, seeming like tiny specks of humanity.

Rafe takes my hand and leads me off the tram. Dozens of steel ladders and ascensi line the terminal platform. We go to the nearest ladder and wait for our turn to descend. Rafe goes first, and I follow.

When I reach the stony ground, Rafe activates his holodigit. When a small, red light flashes above his hand he says, "Follow me."

As we descend the steps, the light on his device changes from red to white. When we're at the halfway point, the light begins to flash.

"How close to the performance platform are we that the light is not yet green, Rafe?"

"Close enough for you to enjoy your favorite performers."

I follow him to the front row when the light glows bright

green then issues a high-pitched beep. He waves his hand over the moss-covered seats, and the beeping stops.

First row. Middle of the platform.

"Would you care for a liquid treat of some sort, Rayne?"

"Just hold on there, sir," I grin. "First you surprise me with these passes, and now I find out these are our seats? How did you possibly get them four days ago?"

"I might have secured them much earlier than that. Only the best on your final month as a subordinate citizen."

"Rafe," I say, my mouth almost too wide to form words, "Thank you. I mean it. This is the best gift *ever.*"

"Anything for you. Now, what would you like for a liquid treat?"

"I would love a violet nectar."

"Stay here. I will go fetch it." As he turns to leave, he stops and says, "Actually, why do you not accompany me?"

I follow his line of sight to see Jhonis, Diamond, and four of their comrades a few rows back.

"I will be fine, Rafe. Go."

He nods and lifts a hand to point at them, his face contorted into a scowl. He lowers his hand and leaves, periodically glancing over his shoulder.

When I lose sight of him beyond the massive rock wall, I tilt my head to the sky. A brisk wind brushes my face. I close my eyes and bask in it. Voices begin to cheer, and I open my eyes to see why. Waving lights the colors of the rainbow illuminate the stage, and I feel the sensation of jitters. As the voices resonate in the amphitheater, I see Rafe returning with our liquid fare.

"My lady," he says as he hands me a small, wooden container.

I hold it to my nose and inhale its sweet aroma. I take a sip, and the liquid warms my throat. I take another, and I feel myself becoming giddy. Suddenly, I feel ready to confide.

"Sir Rafe," I begin.

"Yes, my lady?"

"You have not yet told me your thoughts on the ancient stump."

"It is something of pure mystery. Is it true your mater has not yet spoken of it?"

"She has not."

The lights illuminating the performance platform dim. The sea of voices unites in unbridled glee. I toss my head to the sky and release a few euphoric shouts of my own. The platform remains empty, yet we all know the performers will appear soon.

I take another sip of the warm liquid and say, "I do not require my mater to solve this mystery."

The lights extinguish. The voices grow louder.

He regards me with a playfulness spiked with confusion. Perhaps he thinks the violet nectar influences my words. He presses his forehead to my temple so I clearly hear him say,

"Do share."

"It was *I*, Rafe."

He studies my lips as I speak. Amidst the raucous roar of the crowd, he must not have heard me.

I turn my head and shout to his ear, "I say it was I who—"

Amplified chords on a violin reverberate through the amphitheater, sending the crowd into an even greater height of frenzy. Through billows of smoke, streams of fuchsia and gold lights wave across the performance platform, spilling onto the rows of seats. As the chords increase in volume and speed, silhouettes appear in the smoke. The crowd screams in delighted fury.

The smoke clears, and there stand the Daughters of Lennon, a mere few meters in front of me. The four females are clad in black with splashes of their signature colors of fuchsia, white, azure, and gold. From the first note, I forget my concerns. I forget Rafe.

The violinist, Taya, moves to the edge of the stage atop tall, golden foot soles. I watch her, mesmerized, as she walks upon them effortlessly, losing herself in a rhythmic sway. Her sleeveless top hangs low on her waist in light, synthetic fringes which dance with her every move. Her violin invigorates my senses, sending a wave of chills through me.

The low, smoky sounds of the cello forms a fierce, yet beautiful melody with the violin. The cellist, Misa, sits on a metal seat to the left of the stage. Her long sleeves extend to cover her hand, leaving only her fingers exposed. With each note she plays, her fingers dance as her bow hand strokes the strings with a passionate flow. As her body rocks with the rhythm, her white-streaked hair flips and sweeps about her in a mad swirl.

When they complete the first piece, the crowd roars with a unified voice. It saturates the air until the next piece begins. It's a quicker, louder, more chaotic rendition of a piece we all know from Primary: a sonata from an Ancient named Wolfgang Amadeus Mozart. He may not have belonged to our species, but his musical genius is irrefutable.

The amplified sounds of the bassist, Yari, is the feature of this melody, with her deep, pulsing rhythm. She jumps and rocks at the center of the platform, her azure-colored braids whipping about as she flings her head in time with the rhythm.

The three instruments flood my senses. It's a short piece, and there are no vocals. It makes no difference to the fourth member, Akira, who stands next to the bassist, energizing the crowd with her sultry sway. Her top cuts off at her ribs and hangs to the base of her bottoms in long, shimmery strips of fuchsia and white.

She jumps in time with the beat, clutching a long, steel pole for support. Its base is flat and the top curves into a clear, circular orb. It's the tool through which her vocal magic flows.

I pump my fist in time to the rhythm and melody. The

piece ends, and my ears ring from the cheers of the crowd and the strain of my own voice.

The platform goes black as a thick wave of smoke billows toward us. Then in the darkness, we hear her voice. It's a long and glorious soprano note. It lingers on the air and dances with the smoke. A single, white light illuminates, pouring from above and revealing only her. Everyone goes silent. The only sound is the wind and her voice. It fluctuates between light and airy and sonorous and brooding. It's bold and alluring. It's enchanting and mesmerizing.

The slow, clipping beats of the bass join her, then the violin and the cello. Voice and instrument are united.

I lose myself in their harmony, thrusting my hands in the air. I knock over my vessel, splashes of my drink falling down my leg. I crouch to wipe it off, planting my hand on the moss seat to steady myself.

The music pounds in my chest. I'm so riveted that I can't move. My hand burrows into my seat, and my hand grows cold. Moss sprouts around my hand, growing thick and wide. I try to stand, but my knees are weak. I feel Rafe clutching me under my arms to help me, my fingers still grazing the moss. The higher he lifts me, the higher the moss grows, until my last fingertip slips off it.

I look up to see Rafe's mouth open wide, his eyes wet with disbelief. I look around, hoping no one saw what I just did. Everyone's attention is on the stage, except one person:

Diamond.

11

The light of the morning sun nudges me awake. I roll to my side and stretch before lowering my feet to the ground. I try to suppress the image of Rafe's shocked expression when he saw what I did.

During the return trip, I knew he wanted to say something, but there were too many listening ears. I acted like I didn't notice. Instead, I leaned against the glass, imagining myself hurtling through space at lightning speeds.

When I meet him at midday, I'll have to urge him not to tell my parentes what he saw. Learning about my first ability brought enough strife. I don't want to upset them anymore than I have, now that our relations are improving.

I indulge in a smile when I recall returning to my villa last night: their chamber light quickly extinguishing; entering my chamber to the suspicious scuffling sounds in their own.

I find myself eager to greet them this morn and to experience this day. It is *dies Hypatia*, and there are no discussions at Institute. Instead, it's a day for physical activities. I decide to go to the Tank. I dress myself in my midnight-blue wet suit, made of a light-weight, synthetic rubber. It's quite comfortable to wear whether dry or submersed in water.

Next I step onto my black swim soles which are fit for walking, yet lightweight for swimming. As I exit my chamber, I hear voices in the culina. They speak softly, and their words are rushed. The closer I get, the quieter they become.

Their conversation ceases the moment I enter the room. My stomach swoons at the aroma.

"Dear Rayne, greetings and love this fair morn."

"Yes, a pleasant morn to you, Rayne."

"A good morn to you both," I say, supplanting my curiosity with a smile.

"I see you plan to pass this day at the Tank. Before you do so, your pater and I would be delighted to dine with you. I have made duck eggs and salmon. We are eager to hear whatever you wish to share of your night." My mater offers a smile which is laced with the most fleeting expression of concern.

"Of course," I say.

"Let us convene on the veranda then, shall we?" my mater

suggests. She waves her hand to open the barrier. When I step outside, I see she has already lain out our utensils and plates.

"I will return momentarily with our fare. Please pardon my absence."

My pater slides my chair from the table and beckons for me to sit. I do with a feeling of lightheadedness. It comes from this simple gesture and his willingness to be close to me.

"So my dear, I trust you experienced a night of respectable frivolity?"

"Yes, Pater. As promised, Rafe escorted me here at a descent hour, a thing which I know you are already aware."

"Yes, well, we only meant to ensure you would receive adequate rest for this your day of physical activity." He pauses as his head flickers in the direction of the culina. He clasps his hands, hunches his shoulders, and clears his throat.

"Pater? Is there something you wish to share?" My voice becomes strained with worry. I don't understand this sudden shift in his behavior. I wonder if our good nature has made him uncomfortable. I almost hope it's the case until I force myself to recall their whispering. It's definitely something more.

The air is thick with words meant to destroy my new-found happiness. I sense it. By the submissive manner in which he refuses to meet my gaze, I know it's true.

"Do tell me now, lest I think the worst, Pater."

I turn toward the threshold, wondering why my mater is

taking so long. I can see her slowly moving from one spot to another. She's listening.

My pater rubs his hands together as his lips part, then at last he speaks. "My dear, I do hope you will understand the words I must now say." He doesn't look at me. His eyes remain fixed on his hands as if they contain the right words. "Please know your mater and I truly understand your need to be like your age peers. We are aware of the emotional strife you have endured all these years and how much you must be wishing to declare your latent ability to all whom you encounter."

He pauses. My throat is too dry, and my lips are too stiff to respond.

"We are also aware you are eager for us to register you with the Board." His eyes flicker to the threshold. My mater is still there, feigning final preparations.

"My dear." His throat is hoarser than before, and I sense utter regret. Now I'm truly afraid. "Your desire to be registered is warranted." Again he pauses.

When I hear the faint clearing of a throat from the culina, I can no longer tolerate his hesitancy.

My burning eyes fixed on the table, my voice strains to say, "Pater, whatever you wish to share with me, say it now. *Please.*"

My mater steps onto the veranda, carrying a platter. Her eyes are soft with remorse as she arranges the fare on the table and speaks in a tone to match my pater's.

"I am certain you have heard what occurred with the ancient stump," she says. "Everyone in the colony is distraught with how it could have grown into a tree, seemingly in the course of a single day. Given what we witnessed…with you and the master eagle…your pater and I would like to know…"

She looks to my pater to continue. He brushes his hands through his hair and says, "Was it you who flourished the Pine?"

He's expression is soft with no traces of accusation. But they know. Of course they know. I'm relieved.

"Yes, it was I. I planned to tell you, but I feared how you would respond. I did not want to worry you any more than you already were."

"It is our place to worry about you, Dear Rayne," my mater says. She glances at my pater, and I know there's more.

"Your mater is right. We worry about you, as is our duty. It is also our duty to protect you. As such, we fear for you as to how the Board might respond if they know it was you. So, I regret to say, your mater and I have decided we cannot tell the Board anything about what has happened to you these past few days. To do so may put you at risk."

"What? Risk for what? Why are you afraid?"

"We are afraid because *my* parentes always warned me to be. I do not know their reason, because they never said. But I have listened to them all my life, and I will continue to do so."

"Forgive us, Rayne," my pater says, "but none can ever know about your abilities. It is best you never perform them again. It is the safest course. Also, you must never again fly with the master eagle. We cannot risk someone seeing you."

I don't believe what I'm hearing. Everything is ruined. Never fly again? I refuse to agree to that. And if they won't register me, the Board will have no reason to come.

"Do you not want to learn why this is happening to me? Maybe the Board knows. Maybe they can give us an explanation."

"Rayne, please understand we cannot do that. Our decision is final."

"Again, Pater, what are you so afraid of? What everyone will think? Is that it?" I shriek, planting my hands on my lap to hide the trembling. I ball my hands into fists and study my whitening knuckles.

"It is true the knowledge of this would cause a tumultuous reaction throughout this colony. We do not wish to upset anyone."

"Yet you upset *me*. You care more for the feelings of others than you do your own filia? Or I should say, filia adopted."

The sound of a shattering platter on the ground is enough for me to know the impression my words have left on my mater. She stoops to pick up the pieces as my pater speaks.

"I claim full responsibility for whatever compelled you to declare such a thing. I doubt you will believe my words, but please know *your* words are unjust. Please, Rayne. It is not simply a matter of pretenses. We simply do not know how the Board would view this situation. We do not know how they would react once they learned of your…anomaly."

"How are you so convinced there is no one else out there like me? What proof do you have? Surely there has to be someone else in this realm, or in other realms. *Somewhere* on this Earth."

"There is no way for us to know. However, it is moot. We trust in the wisdom of your mater's parentes. It is best for us to heed their advice."

"Without even knowing why they said it? You want me to heed the advice of people I never met? It is not as though I can ask them. They are *dead.*"

My mater breaks into a sob, and I know I've said too much.

My face is hot with disappointment. As my tears spill to the table, I can only see a blur of distorted shapes. The breeze carries the scent of our fare to my nose, but I've lost my appetite. And if I stay here any longer, I'll say something else to make this worse.

"Forgive me, Mater. I should not have said such a thing."

I don't wait for their response as I push out my chair. My feet lead me into the culina, my eyes too flooded to see. I cross the threshold of my chamber and fling my hand over the panel to seal myself within the confines of my walls.

I pace the floor, my head pounding in defeat. I hear a knock. I ignore it. Instead I tap my fingers, and through a haze of tears I manage to say, "Call Rafe."

His image appears in the bright field before me, and I gaze into his piercing brown eyes. It's as though he looks through me. He doesn't see me here in my chamber. It's not him. It's only his likeness.

"Rafe, if you receive this before you begin your day, please meet me…" Where?

I struggle to mask the anguish in my voice—on my face—as I say, "Meet me in the place of the ancient stump. Please, Rafe. I must see you."

I stare at the field, unsure what else to say. I have no more words. I tap my fingers, and the field disappears.

The voices of my parentes accompany another knock. They've never done this before, so I decide to do something new as well.

I turn to my window threshold and wave my hand to retract the barrier. I swing my legs through the frame and hop to the ground. My shaky legs make me feel like I have leapt a great distance. I sink my hands into the soil to regain my balance then stand to my feet and run. I ignore the growling in my stomach. As I urge my feet to my destination, I fear he'll react the same as my parentes. Or worse. I fear he'll reject me entirely.

12

The smell of lilac and juniper berries floats on the wind. I turn in the direction of the scent I crave. He gazes at me atop his zephyr-mobile, making no effort to mask his concern.

"Thank you for meeting me here," I say, fighting tears.

The place where we meet is a fitting spot. We're in the presence of an occurrence which I can neither explain nor understand with logic. I also can't explain what's happening to me.

"Of course I came, Rayne."

He leaps to the ground, and I study the sound of his feet landing gracefully on the forest floor. I hear his breath growing louder as he approaches me. My cheeks flush as he holds my hands in his. I refuse to meet his gaze. Instead, I rest my forehead on his shoulder and close my eyes. I don't want this moment to end.

Yet, it does.

He nudges me backward so he can see my face. I can't fight his eyes which seek my own. I can no longer suppress the anguish within me.

My breath catches as I force my words from my throat, waving a hand at the Great Pine. "My parentes know what I did."

"I see," he says, the gentle release of his breath almost lost in the rustling of leaves. "Obviously they did not react well. Tell me what I can do to mend it."

I look up at him, surprised he's offering to help me, surprised he doesn't just want to turn and run.

He rests his hands on my arms, almost timidly, then places his forehead to mine. "Rayne."

There's something he wants to say. I can sense it in his halting breath. Instead he lowers his head as if his eyes are desperate to meet my own. I don't oblige. I have no desire for him to see my tears.

"What did they say?"

When I don't answer, he releases a slight groan and pulls me closer. "Might I say something?" he asks. His voice is soft and tender, almost pleading.

I nod, my eyes fixed on the curve of his neck.

"What I saw with the moss was...and this Great

Pine…You flourished it in the course of minutes, hours, it makes no difference. Both instances are unprecedented."

He sighs, and the scent of mint lingers at my nose. I focus on it as I try to avoid the truth: he doesn't know what to think of me. I speak before he has a chance to confirm it.

"My parentes just told me I can never tell anyone else what has happened to me. They also forbid me to fly with the master eagle or perform my abilities at all."

I say the words without emotion. As I watch his arms fold across his chest, my body tightens with emptiness. Only moments before I found solace in the comfort of his embrace. Now I'm barred from it. I lift my face as he turns from me.

"Rayne…" His hesitation bothers me. It's the same as my pater on the veranda.

"This is what I am called."

He lowers his head and sighs, and I feel my lungs deplete of oxygen. My face grows hot as I stand there, staring at his back, believing I've lost him. His shoulders rise and fall, and without turning to face me, he speaks. "I believe you understand my position on the matter, or else your tone would not be as coarse as it is now."

"Take care, Rafe, lest I assume your convictions are again in stride with my pater."

"I assure you I am ever the undogmatic being you have always known me to be—"

"I wonder if I have ever known you at all."

"Do not say such things." He faces me now and attempts to hold my hand, but I retreat. I don't desire his touch.

"Why do you behave in this manner, Rayne? This is unlike you."

"Unlike me? You have it wrong, Rafe, since I can be none other than myself."

"You behave cruelly toward me, when all I mean is to—"

"Now I am cruel?"

"I misspeak. Not cruel. Your behavior is churlish."

I retreat a few steps from the blow, shaking my head as if I didn't hear him correctly. "I think you mean to call me a—dare I speak the word?"

"Do not accuse my mouth of possessing the ability to utter that foul word. I am *not* Jhonis." His eyes, normally soft and inviting, are consumed with a fire which I don't recognize. I have angered him, and I don't care. He has angered me.

"Then let us forget it, Rafe, so we may address the real issue. Tell me now. Are your sentiments in line with my parentes? Do you agree I should hide the truth of who I have become? Do you think I should never again fly. Or are you a comrade of mine?"

"*Rayne.* This matter is not as simple as you demand. You must understand the implications for announcing your ability—*abilities*. The implications of what you have done with this tree alone is enough to send the foundation of all we hold firm and true to the depths of uncertainty—"

"Then rebuke me for causing anyone the *grief* of uncertainty!"

"*No.* By all the stars in the universe, do not twist my words, Rayne."

"Then take care to choose them wisely. Do not squander my devastation on such a trivial word as uncertainty."

"To the deepest depths of my being, I regret uttering it. It was in error. Rayne…please. I beg of you. I know you understand my sentiments. I also know you are too wrought with disappointment to heed them. Please, Rayne. Consider who we are. What we are. Then consider the thing of wonder which none before you have accomplished. Now I beg of you to forget for one moment each time you uttered a whisper to whatever creature crossed your path, each time you soared with the master eagle—It is a miracle unto itself none have witnessed you in flight."

He pauses and stares at me. Never before have I seen him look at me with eyes so wide and strained with frustration. I can't bear to see him look at me this way, so I turn from him.

When he continues, his voice sounds more pleading than ever. "Forget for one moment those experiences are yours. Imagine they belong to someone else. Imagine how unbelievable it would seem to you. How impossible. How much would you question the veracity of it? How much would you fear the person claiming to have accomplished such feats? I beg of you, Rayne, see this from a perspective other than your own.

If you were like us, you would react as we do."

"*If* I were like you?"

"*Rayne.* Is that the only aspect on which you settle your thoughts?"

"It is the truest sentiment you have ever shared with me. You consider me separate from you, when I always regarded us as the truest of comrades. Now I know it was false. You look upon me as they all do, as someone who is beneath you." I spit the words, my mouth writhing in malice.

"You speak with no sense of logic."

"Then call me Sape as those who feel only loathing for me do, and no longer will you be forced the degradation of associating with me."

"You have gone mad! You heed nothing I say. You only wish to quarrel."

"I wish to do more than quarrel, Rafe. I wish never to see you again."

"You do not mean such hasty words, Rayne. Please cease with this impetuousness so we may resolve this matter."

"And how might we resolve a thing when you continue to refer to my just emotions as mad and impetuous?"

"*Rayne.*" He rubs his hands on his face as though he experiences a great, physical pain. "Rayne. If you heed only one thing this day, let it be this. I do not expect you to agree with my position. I merely need for you to understand it as I understand yours."

My hands ball into fists. The fury I feel is not because I don't agree. It's because I do. It's because I understand him precisely, just as I understood my parentes' sentiments. I'm furious because I'm me. I will always be *the other.*

Whether he misspoke or not, Rafe still uttered the most crushing words in all this. He referred to me as someone who is not like him. In his eyes, I will always be different. I will always be a mystery. I will always be a freak.

It was a mistake to have confided in him.

Through burning tears, I hear myself speaking with a voice hoarse with rage. "Depart from me now, Rafe. If ever I set eyes upon you, if ever I hear the sound of your voice or feel the weight of your embrace, I will consider myself plagued. I already possess a pater. I cannot tolerate another in the form of someone I considered my only comrade. As such, I can no longer tolerate you."

I run from him, my body quivering from the implications of my words. I find myself clouded by anger at my own existence, and I've unfairly applied it to him.

Regardless, he doesn't understand. I don't even understand. I'm baffled as to why any of this is happening to me. I'm angry with myself for being so fierce with him when I know he speaks logic. He speaks truth.

I try to calm my rage. Anger will serve no purpose. It will provide no answers.

I possess three abilities, and I will never learn why. My

parentes have barred my access to the Board. They have barred my access to answers. This is my position in life. I'm not like them. I'll never be like them, and I must endure the reality of it alone.

13

My feet lead me westward, and I follow. I know where I wish to go, where I can be oblivious to the world outside its walls. It's what I intended upon waking this morn, and I desire to be there even more.

I run until I see a few horses grazing in the open space of the forest. A spotted brown mare is the first to acknowledge me. I mount and lead her to my destination at a swift pace. When we arrive, I leap to the ground and stroke her neck. "Thank you for your graciousness, Mare." She offers a neigh before trotting in the direction we came.

The colossal structure of the Tank towers above me. A series of ropes, bungees, and zip lines are the means to descend. The most efficient way to access the summit is to climb one of the slanted ladders of steel dispersed between the ropes.

I grab onto the bottom rung, and with each step, I feel my anger subsiding. I reach the undulating wave of the summit and climb onto the rim of smooth pebbles and river rock.

Dozens are present who have come from neighboring colonies. I don't recognize most of them. It's why this is my place of solitude and serenity. Most don't know who I am, and it's easy to avoid those who do. Underwater, I can hear no taunts.

I sit on the rocky surface and dip my feet in the dark, still waters. The crisp cold stings the exposed tops of my feet, but the sun is bright, and the day is warming.

I notice a mater and her infant child. I smile as he squeals and splashes. I watch them for a time, swishing the water with my legs.

I push off the rocks and wade into the lake until I clear the gradual slope of the structure. I dip my head below the surface and dive. The coldness invigorates my face. It refreshes me.

I use my limbs to propel myself deeper. Species of trout, salmon, and whitefish swim past me, brushing my legs in my descent.

As I sink, strobes of white light appear below me. Other divers are here too. I need to illuminate my path, so I drag my fingers through the water and press my thumb and index finger together. I count to three and release them, and a white light shines before me. I point my hand downward to gauge my distance from the bottom. I'm close.

My lungs are still fresh when I reach the lake floor. I extend my hand and brush the green, synthetic surface. It's coated with a fine layer of algae, enough to feed the creatures of the lake. Though the water is dark, it's clear. The aquamarists perform their duty well.

I position my legs beneath me and try to remain still. My suit wishes to carry me upward, so it's difficult to do. I take a few, floating steps before deciding I must return to the surface to replenish my lungs. The higher I ascend, the brighter the rays of the sun become. I flip onto my back and float to the top, and the fresh air splashes my face.

I hear voices around me. Still floating on my back, I lift my head to see if I'm in their path. When I see who it is, I wish I ignored them.

A few meters from me are Diamond and her comrade Pike. It's obvious the two have been discussing me. Pike stares at me, her eyes narrowed and her mouth pursed in animosity. She turns to whisper to Diamond who avoids looking at me, her expression haughty as usual.

I have no desire for confrontation, so I hold my breath and dive. I'm halfway to the bottom when I notice Pike swimming, her graceful strokes intent on reaching me.

I allow her the opportunity. Down here she can make no snide comments. The most she can do is glare.

I look up to see Diamond diving toward us. Her shoulder-length hair flows in her face with each downward stroke, giving her an ethereal appeal. She taps Pike on her shoulder. Pike shakes her head in response, and I'm baffled as to what she thinks she can accomplish.

I stare at Pike, challenging her either to act or leave me to myself. I swim closer, and she retreats a few strokes. She didn't expect me to do that.

I'm already weary of this, so I shift my feet beneath me, lift a hand, and wave my fingers at them to say good day. I spread my arms and legs upward, and I begin to sink to the lake floor. I continue until my feet brush the slick surface.

I fan my arms about me to hold my position. I'm dancing with the flow of the lake, feeling myself at one in its depths. My lungs feel fresh, like I could remain down here forever. I smile from a peace which only this depth can bring.

Diamond and Pike watch me as they gradually retreat to the surface. As I notice their eyes widening, so does my smile. Then Diamond pauses in her ascent and points to the surface. Why she shows concern for me, I neither know nor care. My lungs don't burn.

She continues to swim upward, periodically looking down at me. From the chopping motion of her upward strokes, it's almost as if she fears my resolve.

She's too far above me now for me to see her clearly. I want to reactivate my light, but my fingers feel too stiff and cold to move. I wish I wore my swim gloves.

I allow my hands to drift in the coldness, testing to see

how long I can tolerate it. I wave my arm in front of me so I can see my hands, and I become mesmerized by the movement. I almost don't notice the legs above me as divers propel themselves to the surface. I'm at the bottom alone.

Now I watch as the last of the swimmers break the surface and swim toward the rim. I wonder the cause for this, yet I don't pursue. I'm down here alone, and it's peaceful.

The serenity compels me to close my eyes. I feel cold, yet warm. It's as though the coldness circulates within me, and my body suit insulates me from the temperature of the water engulfing me.

Still, the water seems to penetrate my suit and my flesh. It flows through me. I visualize my lungs filling with oxygen and marvel in the serenity of being alone in the Tank for the first time. I imagine I can remain here forever.

I wave my arms and try to hold my legs firmly in place. Strangely, they obey. The more I move my arms to steady myself, the less it feels I need to do so. My arms are so used to being down here that they now feel free from the tug of the waves. They no longer seem like they're floating but weighted as though I hold them up against the force of gravity.

My flesh becomes acclimated to it as well. The water gives the sensation of a breeze. My lungs feel fresher now, and I imagine they're filling with oxygen.

I imagine the rise and fall of my chest as if I'm breathing underwater. I'm so focused on this that it's like I stand motionless, and my feet are on solid ground.

My suit no longer seems flooded from the depths of the lake. Instead, it feels like drops of water trickle down my body, landing on the exposed tops of my feet.

Warmth meets my face, as if the rays of the sun seek me down here, warming me, invigorating me, encouraging me to remain. Even my hands feel warmer. It all feels so authentic that I open my eyes.

A terrifying chill strikes me. What I see can't be real.

The dozens of swimmers are all gathered on the rim, staring down at me. I shift my eyes from them to the slope of the concrete structure. It's no longer submersed. There's no water around me or above me. There's only a shallow puddle beneath my feet as the water from my suit drips on the synthetic surface.

My mind betrays me. It suffers from oxygen depletion. The vision seems so real that I know I'm in danger. I need someone to rescue me from my airless prison. I can't move to free myself.

The sky darkens, and they're all pointing. Not at me. They point behind me and above me.

Where's Diamond? Why does she not return for me to wake me from this nightmare?

I realize my arms are still extended at my sides. I lower them slightly, and an icy gust of watery wind strikes my back and rains down on me. My instinct tells me to raise them again.

The showers cease.

I close my eyes and breathe, knowing I only do so in my mind. I hear shouts from the rim. I also hear what sounds like cresting water and the flapping of fins.

The only way to break myself from this vision is to move. I must see what they all see. I must confront whatever is behind me.

Slowly I turn. What I behold sends my body pulsing on the verge of hysteria. A massive wave looms behind me, trapping in it the flopping bodies of fish desperate to break free. It towers above the rim of the Tank, blocking the light of the sun.

As my arms fall to my sides, I open my mouth, and I scream. My eyes widen in terror as the wave crashes on me in a fury. It stings my flesh like shards of glass, tossing me like I'm a leaf. I can't close my mouth or my eyes. I can no longer scream.

I feel my lungs beginning to burst.

14

Blotches of green and mahogany appear above me. Arms quaver and pulsate over my chest. The water which was once drowning me now seeks release through my mouth. I gag and roll to my side, coughing and tearing in the relief that I'm not dead.

The colors become more defined. They're not blotches I see, but a wet mass of green-streaked hair. Diamond has saved me.

She waves her arms and flings them to her side. My throat seizes, and I cough with a sickening force as the last drops of water leave my body. My shoulders rise and fall as quickly as my breath. My eyes are filled with tears, but I can see her. She stares at me with an expression which I'm too disoriented to decipher. I shift to my forearms and notice Pike with her.

When my breathing slows and the flow of my tears cease, Diamond speaks. "You are revived. The conscience of my duty is clear. Take care, Rayne. If astonishing events continue to occur in your presence, we might begin to think you proof of a thing called cursed."

Pike tossed her head in annoyance and stands to leave. Then Diamond leans over me and whispers, "Take care not to expose yourself."

Without further word, she stands to her feet and walks away as she wrings the water from her hair. Pike follows her, glancing over her shoulder at me.

Dripping and shivering from fright, I try to wrap my mind around her words. I begin to notice others present. Dozens of swimmers now surround me. A flood of comments and questions rains upon me.

"Are you fully mended now, young citizen?"

"You must beg our forgiveness for failing to realize you were trapped."

"Your foot was caught, was it not?"

"You are quite fortunate a medicum was in our midst. Is it true you reside in the same zone?"

"Ah! The two of you must be the best of comrades."

"Yes. How mirificus for your comrade to be the source of your rescue. I am certain this event shall bind you for life."

Their words are too much for me to bear. I stumble to rise to my feet and feel gentle hands supporting me in assistance.

"Take care, young citizen. Are you certain you are quite well enough to stand?"

I turn to each of them, forcing my shivering mouth into a smile. "Thank you for your concern. All of you. I assure you I am fine. Now I fear I must catch…Diamond…to thank her properly. Do pardon me. Again, thank you all."

I politely squeeze through them, my legs shaky from the trauma. Diamond and Pike have not yet descended the rim, so I force my feet to a jittery trot to catch them. Regardless of our relations, I owe her my words of gratitude. I also have to find out if there was any hidden meaning behind her words.

As I near them, I hear their conversation. They don't notice I'm behind them.

"Why did she not follow us all? Surely she cannot be so daft. I heard a few people stating they believed she must have been trapped between a few sunken rocks. Also, why would an aquamarist and aerisma have convened this morn —when the lake was occupied by dozens—to conduct whatever act they meant to accomplish? Do you think the aquamarist meant to try some superfluous method of purifying the lake? It makes no sense. Regardless, surely they must have known how dangerous their act would be. Again, why would they have done such a thing in the presence of swimmers? There is no logic to any of it."

"Pike, I assure you I am as ignorant of all this as are you."

"Then let us seek them for answers. Have you spotted them? Where must they be now? Surely they know what they caused. Surely they know their dutiful zeal nearly resulted in—dare I say—*death*. How could they have been so careless, regardless of whether it was only that Sape?"

The blow from the word forces me to stop. I no longer listen. I no longer follow. There's no need to offer my words of gratitude. They will fall on deaf ears. She didn't save me for concern. There was no secret message. She only rescued me because her dutiful conscience compelled her.

As I watch them climb over the rim to descend, I can't stop thinking, if only they knew. There was no conducting of experiments, no collaborative efforts. I did this, yet I have no idea how.

Once again, I don't know what to think or how to explain this to myself. All I know is I forced a body of water to stand tall and firm.

Pike spoke true. There's no single ability which could perform the wave feat—no single *person* who could do so.

I find myself shivering but not from the cold. It's from something I'm beginning to realize. This incident could be an extension of what occurred on the Annex. The idea leads me to suspect something else. I'm anxious to confirm, but I need to wait until I'm alone.

Those on the rim have already begun their descent in search of answers. I watch as they vacate then trot around the rim, peering over the edge as I go. Gradually, they all disperse, though I suspect I don't have much time before another round of swimmers arrives.

I'm not certain exactly what to do. I trust my instincts to guide me. I press my hands onto the rocky rim, ignoring the digging sensation in my knees. I don't know if I should close my eyes or keep them open. I choose to stare at my hands, relaxing and concentrating on summoning a force which I might not even possess.

The rocks feel cool on my palms. The longer I hold them there, the opposite of what I expect happens. The ground grows cold when the heat from my palms should be warming it. My *palms* grow cold. The feeling becomes more intense, yet it doesn't bother me. The coldness comes from within me.

My hands begin to vibrate as the ground shifts and pulses. I feel it in my teeth. It's alive with a seismic activity which shouldn't exist in this place. It happens because I cause it. It's one facet of the four elements, and I've just executed it.

Terracostos: Earth.

I lift my hands to my face and press them to my cheeks. They're ice cold. I lift my hands above my head, reaching to the sky. This time I close my eyes. I wave my fingers, and a slight breeze brushes my face. I wave my hands, and a gust of wind washes over me.

I open my eyes again and stand to my feet. I spread my fingers and wave my arms around me. A torrent of wind blows on the surface of the lake, sending it crashing. The wind encircles me, but it doesn't seize me. I'm encapsulated in a bubble of warmth, while the fury of the winds swirls around me.

I hold my arms and hands steady now, lifting them slowly to the sky. The wind changes its course upward, dragging with it the crest of the lake and the pebbles on the rim. Higher and higher they rise until I'm surrounded by a wall of water and earth.

I drop my arms, and the pebbles and crest land with a resounding crash and splash.

Aerisma: Air.

My skin tingles in ecstasy as I search the rim for what I think I need. There's no need to test water. I need to try the last. I crave it.

I run along the rim to ensure none have witnessed the winds I caused. No one ascends. As I'm about to retreat from the edge, I notice a frayed section of a rope. I grab it between my fingers and pull. The twine doesn't come loose, and I have nothing to use to cut it.

I imagine my fingers searing the tips. The twine breaks free. I hold it up to inspect the charred end. Though this confirms the last, it's not enough for me.

I enclose it in my palms, imagining the twine becoming

red with flames. Smoke seeps through the tiny gaps in my clasped hands. I part them slightly, and sparks of flames emit. My palms don't burn. They feel comfortably cool.

When I open my hands, the twine is gone, but the flame remains. It feels like a cold, crisp wind. I imagine the temperature growing colder. I imagine myself in the arctic poles, hunting with the great White Bears which once roamed the Earth. I imagine I'm swimming with them in the freezing waters.

I lift my hands to my face to smell them. The scent is of burnt twine. Coldness radiates from the flames, and an invigorating chill stirs within me. It soothes me.

I feel myself spinning as I inhale the juxtaposition of ice and ember. I spread my fingers to stroke the imaginary polar beast. I feel its presence with me and within me.

Now I sense myself running—or swimming. I can't tell which. I only feel the iciness blanketing me as I move. I allow my eyes to inform me. When I open them, all I see is orange and red dancing around the circumference of the rim, in a towering wall of flames.

As I behold what I have done, the fourth element surrounds me.

Fire is all I see.

Ignitor.

Tears arise, but they dissolve before they find a path to my cheeks. Though I'm engulfed by flames, I'm not hot. Instead the beat of my heart slows, and my breath constricts. I'm on the verge of hypothermia. I sink to the ground and huddle into a ball. My teeth chatter, and my muscles twitch as I try to expel the warmth of my breath onto my huddled form.

I lie still not thinking, just waiting for the sensation to pass. Gradually, my jaw and muscles relax. The shivering subsides, and I feel my lungs replenishing.

I don't know how long I've been here like this when the heat of the sun warms me. When I hear grunts and chatter from people ascending the Tank, I know it's time to leave.

I stand to my feet, feeling like I need to rip the suit off me or drench myself in the lake, but I dare not. Instead I decide to cool myself in my choice of descent.

A few meters ahead is a small structure of steel which is secured deep into the surface of the rim. Attached to it is a harness which hangs from cables. I secure myself in the harness, take a couple steps in retreat, then push myself off the rim.

I spread my arms as I glide, delighting in the speedy descent. I extend my legs when I'm near the ground, enjoying the final gusts of wind on my face. When my feet touch the soil, I run to slow my momentum before releasing myself from the harness.

No one is in the vicinity of the landing port. I'm alone amidst the trees. I can't resist the desire to cause the ground to rumble, so I do. Just a tiny bit. Just enough to remember. I sink to my knees and press my hands to the soil. As the ground shakes beneath my palms, my mouth retracts into a grin.

I remove my hands and stand to my feet, brushing the soil from my suit. Though my thoughts are a jumble, one thing is certain. I've proven my suspicion to be true. Somehow, I possess all four facets of the elements. Whatever happened on the Annex is part of it, just heightened.

Even greater, I've just discovered I possess six abilities:

Susurrator.

Floresca.

Aquamarist.

Aerisma.

Teracostos.

Ignitor.

As I search for a horse to return to my villa, I remind myself of something. Though ecstatic from this discovery, more than ever I need to know why this is happening.

There's so many questions which need answers: the identity of my parentes of birth; why the Luminescence came 15 years late—twice; why I possess so many abilities; why they're all so powerful.

I decide something. In three weeks, I'll be of age. I'll leave this place and the burden of my secrets. When the day arrives, I'll climb the canopy of trees and search the skies for the master eagle. I'll bid him to carry me east.

If the Board can't come to me, I'll go to them in the Capitolium. There I'll solve this mystery. As for the rest of my days on this Earth, I'll go where no one knows me. I'll seek a new colony, and I'll be reborn.

Until then, I'll whisper to the creatures. I'll share my abilities with the flora. I'll dance with the air, embrace the flood of water, breathe the smell of fire, and recline in the Earth. I'll confide in nature alone and embrace who I have become.

15

I greet the new day with courage and unwavering conviction. Soon I'll have answers. Until then, I must tolerate the time I have left in this colony.

When I enter the culina, my mater is present but my pater is not. She sits at the table, sipping hot tea. The moment I see her, a wave of regret washes over me.

"Good day, Mater."

She turns to face me and offers what seems like a forced smile. "Good day, dear Rayne. I hope the night proved restful for you."

"It did. Mater—"

"You must be terribly famished since you did not have

fare last night."

"Mater, I—"

"Allow me to prepare sustenance for you now. Pardon me for not already having done so."

"You do not have to."

"Yes, I do."

"I can do it myself. There is no need to trouble—"

"I am your *mater*."

She pounds her fist on the table, spilling her tea. She rubs her hand on the surface as if to soothe it from her act.

"Mater…Please. Forgive me. I should not have said those things. I did not even mean them. I was just so angry."

She drags her fingers through the spilled tea, like she's in a trance, then sets her cup on the table with a deep sigh. "I know you did not mean them. Even still…"

"I know. Words can hurt, I regretted them the moment I spoke them."

She looks at me, her eyes red and watery. "It is just… Our relationship has been strained for so many years. When you referred to me as…" She wipes a hand over her eyes and sniffs. "It is fact. I *am* your mater adoptive, but I have never thought of myself as such. To hear you say it…"

"It was the worst thing I could have said to you, and if I could erase it from your memory, I would. It is not how I think of you."

She offers a weary smile and nods.

"I do." She clears her throat and shakes her head as if clearing her thoughts from all this. "We will speak of it no further. And now, you must eat."

I watch as she prepares morning fare for me. The way she moves slowly, as if in a daze, I know this isn't over. There's something else she wants to say.

"Mater? Are you sure you are alright?"

"Now you must believe *me* when I say I am. I am just thinking about what you said about my parentes—your valid question, I mean," she adds lifting a hand to stop me from interjecting.

She sets a plate in front of me, and I inhale the aroma. She was right. I'm starving. I pick up my tool and take the first bite, my guilt not allowing me to savor the taste.

She sits next to me, running her fingers through the wet streaks of tea, not bothering to clean it up. "I realized it was unfair of me to expect you to accept our position without answering your valid questions. So, here it is."

She takes a deep breath, wiping her hand on the table, and says, "My parentes were the Board's age peers, as you know, and their perspective on the Board reflected it. They lived in the Capitolium and served as Stewards. Apparently this is a position given to those whom the Board deemed—as my pater once put it, 'insufficiently ardent.' I do not know precisely what he meant by this. Neither of my parentes ever told me.

"A few years before I was born, the Board allowed them to move to this colony. Eventually, as I neared my seventeenth year, my parentes urged me to remain here with them. Their reason was in the form of a warning. They told me the Board was to be feared, and I was never to tell anyone they said this. I plead with them to tell me why, but they never did. When I married your pater, they warned him too. So now I say the same to you. I am sorry I do not have more to tell you to explain it, but I hope you can at least understand."

I place my utensil on my plate, considering her words. "I do. Thank you for telling me." I take another bite, convinced more than ever that if anyone knows what's happening to me, it will be the Board. I can't say it to her though.

I decide to change the subject. "Where is Pater? I owe him an apology too."

"There is no need. As for his whereabouts, Sir William begged an audience with him this morn."

My heart leaps to my throat at the declaration. Though I already know the answer, I still ask, "For what purpose?"

"I do not yet know. I suspect he will inform me upon his return."

I don't need to wait. Sir William is Diamond's pater. Diamond must have told him what happened at the Tank and what she saw me do at the concert.

I feel my mater's eyes on me.

"Is something troubling you, Rayne?"

"There was an incident yesterday at the Tank. I believe it is the reason Sir William contacted Pater."

"Incident? Of what sort?"

"Well…those who witnessed it will claim I nearly drowned."

"Drowned? How can this be? You said nothing last night. Why would you not tell us?"

"I was never in danger. And Diamond was there. It was she who revived me."

"You are fortunate she is a medicum, Rayne. How could this have occurred? Oh Rayne, it must have been terrifying. Are you recovered now?"

She brushes her hands over my face and hair to inspect me. The act warms me.

"I *am,* Mater, truly and completely. Do pardon my failure to inform you. As I said, I was never in real danger, so I did not wish to worry you."

"Dear Rayne!" My mater yells, making me jump. "It is my prerogative to worry—both your pater and I. You must vow never to withhold such a thing from us again."

I nod in acknowledgement, knowing that in this moment, my pater and Sir William are talking about what happened. They'll know it had nothing to do with experiments. Though my pater wouldn't dare express his suspicion to Sir William, he'll know I'm the one who caused it. He'll tell my mater, and they'll be even more worried about me. And worse, they'll hate the fact that I tried to hide it from them. Though it's a conversation I don't want to have, there's no way around it. So I tell her.

When I finish, she lowers her head and sighs. She stares at her lap for so long, that I know this is too much for her. "I did not mean for it to happen."

"I know, Rayne. And now…I do not know what to do." Her voice trembles as she shakes her head in defeat.

"I vow to you I will do all I can to ensure something like this does not happen again. If I must confine myself to my chamber until I come of age, I will. If I must live in solitude after that, I will. I am used to being alone after all."

"Dear Rayne, there is no need to declare such things. You could not have known it would happen, and you cannot isolate yourself. There is a solution, and we will discover it together."

She picks up her cup and sips her tea. Though by now it must be lukewarm, she drinks it like it's deliciously hot. She sets it down, drums her fingers on the table, glancing at me as she does.

"Until such time, worry not. Attend to your affairs today as you normally would. Try not to think too much about all of this…if that is even possible. As for me, I must begin my duty for the day. I will see you this eve."

She gets up, her hand brushing my hair as she leaves. I listen to her exiting through the front as I clean my plate. Then I wander down the veranda steps, setting my feet in a brisk stroll toward nothing. I have no place to be, no comrade to meet. All I know is I have to stay away from people. I can't risk something else happening.

I wander through the forest, I'm met with a strange feeling, like a heaviness suddenly weighs my soul. It's a sensation I've never felt before. It feels like death is following me.

Footsteps trample the forest floor behind me. When I turn, I see nothing, yet I know I'm not alone. I walk faster, but I can't escape the feeling, whatever *it* is.

I slow my pace, my breath quickening, and my heart pounding. I feel a shriek rising in my throat. I sink to my knees, pressing my hands to my ears, willing the sensation to subside. Instead it grows stronger, and the sound of trampling grows louder. I rock on my knees, my eyes tightly shut, my hands still pressed to my ears.

The footsteps encircle me. They're so close that I notice something about them. They're stumbling and weak like a timid beast. I hear the breath of a creature. *Creatures.* Not strong, but strained. Desperate.

In a panic, I scramble to my feet and run. I glance over my shoulder to confirm I'm not being followed, and smack into a wall of muscle and smooth fur. I fall to the ground and look up to see a stag. His antlers sway gently as he approaches me. Blood stains his neck. I notice the imprint of my cheek. I lift my hand to wipe my face and find it smeared with his blood.

He lowers his head, and more blood drips to the ground. My eyes trace the source. A narrow branch is embedded in the top of his neck.

I retreat several steps when I notice an elk to my right. Her stance is weak, and her eyes are milky with age. She staggers toward me, her legs betraying her weakness.

More creatures approach. There are 23 of them, and I know them all. These creatures roam my colony, and they have sought me. Now I feel genuine fear, but not because of them.

They wait for me to act, but I can't. I sink to my knees, my body succumbing to a wave of hysteria.

"Leave me be! Luminescence why will you not *leave me be?* Why is this happening? This is too much! I didn't ask for this, and I don't want it. Any of it!"

I bend my knees and bury my head in my lap, listening to their moans. I lift my face, bitterness churning at what my existence has become.

"Why do you seek *me?* Why do you not wander out of this colony and perish in the wild as your kin do? *Go!*" I scream.

They don't leave. They *won't,* not until I act. They belong to our colony. They dwell in these forests and graze among us. They live with us, and therefore they die with us. They die *for* us. They seek our providiors, and now they have sought me.

These creatures need me. They need me to quiet my fear.

They need me to act. I force myself to my feet, my chest pounding.

Though they know the way, they can't knock at the door to their passing. It must be a human hand to do so. There I must go—now, while these kindred beings still live.

16

A six-meter wall of brick stands before me. I lift an anxious hand to knock on a massive door of weathered wood. As the creatures lumber toward me, I wonder what I'll say when the door opens.

It was disconcerting having them follow me here, their various utterances almost begging me to release them from life.

The door lumbers open just wide enough for me to see the dim light inside the structure. It opens a bit wider, and a man of stout, short stature presents himself.

He's older than my parentes by two decades. Though usually only subordinate citizens dye our hair, his natural gray is streaked with bright-blue. He's the man to whom the providiors in our colony go when called to duty. His name is Sir

Theo, and he's the master processor.

He regards me with wonder, which I expect. He pushes the door open, his eyes scanning the creatures behind me. He opens it wider still and steps outside in search of something. He turns to me, his stout jaw struggling to form words to express his confusion.

"So many on this day and with no prior notification?" he mutters. "Femella, why do you stand before me? You know only providiors are permitted access through this door."

He turns from me and wanders to the edge of the forest. "Where are all the providiors who deliver this great number in want of processing?" Again he returns to my side, gazing at me as if he's confounded with drink. "I implore you to tell me, femella. To where have they gone? With this number of ailing herd, I am in want of questioning the providiors who brought them to me without proper notice. Where are they? How is it possible they do not complete their duty? What is this lunacy?"

"There are no other providiors on these grounds, Master Processor."

"Then they have all at once taken ill? It is not possible. How am I to process these creatures in their absence? Femella, tell me what has occurred to cause you to stand here in their stead. I demand an explanation for this insanity."

I don't know how to explain in a way he'll believe, so I keep it simple. "It is I alone who these creatures follow."

"Ah!" He releases a gleeful sigh as he nods and pats me on the shoulder. "I see. Yes, of course. Thank the universe, the confounding cloud has passed."

His hearty laugh feels eerie in the somber scene. He neither looks at me nor the creatures as he revels in his fit of relief. At last he says, "Yes, femella. I shall sleep soundly this night knowing I have misinterpreted this situation. These creatures are not here to be processed." His smile dissolves, and his eyes narrow with sternness. "In such case, femella, I must demand. Why did you knock at this door? What purpose might you have for causing me such unjust alarm?"

"The alarm I cause you is not baseless, I am afraid. What I am to tell you will be impossible for you to believe, Master Processor, yet it is true. It is a secret which I would keep to myself if not for the implications of what it would cause. These ailing creatures sought me out to escort them here."

He looks past me as though he doesn't hear me.

"Master Processor, I implore you to observe their conditions. You will see I speak the truth. *Please.*"

His thick brows rise on his forehead. He wanders in their midst, passing from one to the next. With his back facing me, he speaks with a slight tone of reprimand.

"You claim to have come alone. Then you must tell me at once femella, from whence have you discovered this number of ailing creatures in want of passing? Why did they not do as nature bids if they could find no providior? Or perhaps I should ask why you have intercepted them on their route to seeking dissolution from this world."

He returns to me, his rebuking eyes searching my own for answers. "I urge you to confess why you have done such a thing."

"I am afraid the answer will prove more than you will be able—or willing—to believe. Please just trust when I say I need you—*beg of you*—to allow us entry, Master Processor, so these creatures' lives will not end in futility. They have come this far. Do not suffer them to journey beyond this colony to perish when they sought me."

He clasps his hands behind his back and studies me. His eyes narrow, causing his bushy brows to cast a shadow over them. "You claim it was you whom they sought?"

"I speak only truth."

"How? How can such a thing be so?"

"*Please,* Master Processor. You may question me after, but for now, I implore you to permit them entry. If it is assistance you require, then allow me to do so. You have stated you cannot process them alone."

My heart pounds with desperation. I feel the powerful compulsion of duty coursing through my veins. I can sense their anguish, their impatience, and their longing for death. Their emotions permeate me and become my own. I know we must act now. I won't waver in my conviction regardless of what he believes. I have to ensure their harvesting for the benefit of this colony.

"Master Processor, it is evident you do not trust the integrity of this situation. Regardless, you must allow us entry lest these creatures continue to suffer on their feet. It is your *duty* to do so."

His eyes widen, and his lips flutter from the halted rasp of his breath. Finally he says, "Enter. *Enter.*"

He opens the door to its full width and stands aside, holding out an ushering hand. I step into the spacious, dimly lit room. It's a sacred space. Only the master processor, his harvesters, and the providiors are permitted access.

It's nothing like I guessed it to be. A ceiling of wooden logs towers several meters above my head and meets at a slanted apex. The walls are made of brick and wood. There are no windows. No natural light enters this space.

Along the two main walls are rows of alcoves of uniform size. Some of them contain large, thin sheets of metal which divide the alcoves into smaller spaces. On the floor of each area is a metal grate.

At each end of the room is a stainless steel door. One is much wider than the other. I take a few steps toward the far end. On either side of the steel door are dozens of opaque, white aluminum carts of various sizes, hovering above the floor.

"Make haste, femella!"

I turn to see the master processor moving from space to

space, pressing buttons, one of which illuminates each alcove with a bright light.

"What would you have me do, Master Processor?"

He flails his arms in the air in response, his pace quickening until he reaches the last row. He scampers toward me and plants his hands on my shoulders. "You must direct the creatures where to go, femella. Behold! They await your guidance."

When I turn around, they're all gathered in a bunch, their eyes directed at me. I can feel their weakened states, and it appalls me that my ignorance has caused them to wait.

"How do I accomplish this, Master Processor?"

"Call their names, femella. Have each one follow you to the place fitting of his or her size."

He pauses and compares the number of creatures to the alcoves. "It would seem we are unequally matched. *This* is why I require proper notice to prepare."

He utters a low growl, lifts a hand to scratch the top of his head, and grunts. Then he speaks with an exasperated sigh. "There is no time to adjust the dividers. We shall have to manage. Be on with it, femella. I shall ready myself in the meantime."

Without further word, he trots to the opposite end of the room and pauses at the steel door. He presses his hand on a panel to the right of it. It opens, and he runs into another space, much more brightly lit than this one. In the brief moment I can see inside, I can tell it's much different than this room. It's stark and bright and vacant.

I turn to the creatures, and I know I have no time to be confused. I've been given instruction, and I have to act. I locate the nearest space which is free of dividers.

"Stag, here."

I wave my arms to usher him toward the alcove, and he begins his lumbering and grateful walk. The moment he enters, he lowers himself to the ground in rest. He's waiting for the next step, but I don't know what it is yet. Next I call the elk, running faster this time to lead her to a space.

I do a quick count and almost panic from the number. There are 21 creatures remaining: three geese, five ducks, four pheasants, three sheep, four hares, a boar, and a wolf. I only need glance to know the wolf doesn't belong to this colony. I have no time to consider why he entered the territory of another pack and why he sought me.

There aren't enough small spaces to accommodate the smaller creatures, so I place them all in groups of their species. When I complete my task, I turn to survey them all, panting with anticipation.

"Femella! Now you."

The master processor has returned, and he looks more harried than before. He's dressed in rubber boots which extend to his knees with a tight seal. Latex gloves cover the full length of his arms. A vinyl suit is tucked into both his boots and gloves. He wears a rubbery headpiece which covers his head and neck, with a clear, plastic shield forming perfectly to his face.

"Go *now*, femella," he repeats.

I jerk from his insistence, unsure what to do. "Pardon, Master—"

"We have not the time for ceremony of speech. I need you to do as I say without hesitation. Are you quite capable?"

"Yes. I—"

"Very good. Go through that door there. You see it? Enter there and prepare yourself."

"I do not understand what I am to—"

"You need not do a thing other than cross the threshold and stand on the X. The system shall do the rest. Now off you go, femella. We have no time to waste. Off you go at *once*."

I turn from him and run to the door when he shouts, "Oh, and do remove your foot soles and holodigit before you step onto the X!"

Still confused by his lack of instructions, I mimic his action by pressing my hand to the panel. The steel door swings open to reveal the stark room. My eyes blink rapidly to acquaint themselves to the change in light. In the middle of the hard, glossy floor is a formation of black tiles. They form the letter X.

I pull off my foot soles as I approach it. Then I slip my device off my fingers. The instant I step onto the X, a rectangular, glass box drops from the ceiling. Thick smoke pours into it, making me cough.

My skin tingles and feels simultaneously cold and hot. I wrap my arms around my body when several mechanical wires extend from the ceiling and seize my foot soles and device. Another set tugs at my garments, removing them with the swift ease of a mother to her child.

I'm naked, enclosed in a glass box, in a bright, sterile room. I watch my garments being sucked through tubing which I didn't notice before. The tubes recede into the ceiling, and a wide barrier retracts.

Wires appear through the opening. Suspended from them are the same items which the master processor wears. The back of the vinyl suit is open, and the arms and legs are positioned for me to slip into them. The instant I do, I feel the back of the garment sealing. The boots are lowered to the ground. I step into one of them, and it instantly seeks the heat of my flesh, enclosing the garment within it.

The wires stretch the latex gloves in front of me. When I slip my hands into them, the wires position them on the full length of my arms. Another wire positions the headpiece. In the reflection of the glass, I see it has covered all of my hair.

The final wire lowers a thick, plastic sheet and moves it toward my face. The instant it touches me, it bonds to my skin, sealing my means of breath. Before I can panic, two thick needles extend from the floor and puncture the plastic at the precise location of my nostrils. Oxygen floods into my lungs, and I breathe rapidly from the exhilaration of it.

The glass box lifts to the ceiling, a series of high-pitched beeps sound, and suddenly I hear the voice of the master processor in my ear. "Femella, you must come now."

I hear his voice as clearly as if it's in my head. I realize it comes from a communication chip imbedded in the headpiece. I assume there must also be a means of him hearing me, so I answer. "I will come this instant, Master Processor."

I step off the X, and the steel door swings open. When I enter the processing room, a smoky mist on the air greets me.

"Mind the cart lest I find myself in want of a cremator. *Now* femella, my impatience be pardoned."

As he speaks, one of the larger carts whizzes past me, grazing my sleeve. It glides toward him as he draws his hands to his chest in a smooth, gentle motion. When it hovers next to him, he lowers one arm and waves it with a flourish. He hoists his arm upward, and the stag levitates. He draws his other arm to him, and the cart positions beneath it. He closes one arm on top of the other, and the stag lands gently on the cart.

My eyes water in awe. I knew he was a magnos, yet I have never witnessed him employing his ability. Now I know why. There are a few magnoves in my colony. The master processor uses his ability—wielding the magnetic core of Earth—to make his duty of choice more efficient. I wonder why he would need any assistance from me.

"Femella, to me. You must perform your duty *now.*"

My feet feel like they're glued to the ground. I open my mouth to question, but I hear myself only squeak a single word. "Duty?"

He speaks quickly, yet gently. "I must trust your claim that these creatures sought you. By all the stars in the universe, I do not know how it is so, but such a thing is only possible with the ability of providior. In this moment, we have no choice but to *hope* it is true. You must engage in the ability now, femella."

"How?"

"First, you must relax. Then you must concentrate and do as your instincts guide you."

There's no time to question his instructions. I close my eyes, willing any sense of purpose to flood my senses. The more evenly I breathe, the more my mind clears to what I must do.

I open my eyes, and my feet lead me to the stag. My heart beats in rhythm with his. Somehow I hear it. I feel it. I look into his gentle and imploring eyes. The longer I gaze, the colder my left hand becomes. I'm compelled to place it over his heart.

I press my hand to his chest. My right hand now feels soothingly warm. I place it on him, stroking his face, his muzzle, and his neck. Slowly and gently my right hand brushes him as my left remains planted firmly on his chest.

As the beat of his heart slows, the longing in his eyes wanes, and the sound of his breath quiets.

I stroke his muscular hind as his heart becomes still, and I no longer feel it beating against my cold hand. No longer do I hear the sound of his breath or feel the rise and fall of his chest. I know I can remove my hand. He has passed to the realm of the dead.

"I would not believe it, had I not witnessed it myself. It appears you speak true. You have done good work."

His voice jolts me from my moment of serenity with the creature. His eyes soften, and his mouth curls in a smile. He says nothing more. He flicks his wrist, cups his hands so his fingers meet at the tips, then lowers his arm to the ground.

I hear the sound of thick liquid pouring through the metal grate. I locate the source and gasp at what I see. The blood of the stag flows to the ground in a stream.

We discuss this process at Institute, yet none other than the master processor and providiors have ever witnessed it. As I watch the blood pour through the grate, the moment is eerie yet beautiful.

"Respectu, Madam Providior," he says, his gentle voice once again startling me in my fascination. "How you have come to be so, I shall not question. I am honored to be at your service this day. This is your first, so I shall direct you. However, as long as you allow your instincts to lead you, you shall be in little need of my guidance."

The pace of his speech becomes quicker with each word. I understand why. There are still 22 creatures to process, and we're wasting time with my instruction.

"Now, Madam Providior, I must transfer this creature for harvesting. In my absence, your task is to gage their hearts to determine which we must process next. We must work quickly."

Without further word, he turns to the stag. The flow of blood has ceased. He waves his hands in a flourish, and the cart hovers toward the wider of the two steel doors. It swings open to allow the cart entry to a room similar to this one, only brighter. There's a woman standing there, dressed the same as us. She must be the harvester.

In the briefest of instants, she regards me with confusion. Though her face is covered with a mask, the language of her body is enough.

The door swings closed, and I'm left in dimness, surrounded by near death. The rate of my breath increases. I relax my shoulders, roll my head to stretch my neck, and close my eyes. I envision the creatures waiting in the alcoves.

I hear them. It's not the sounds of their breath but the beating of their hearts. One rhythm beckons me more than the rest, and my feet lead me toward it. My eyes open of sheer desire, and I find myself marching toward the boar. I observe her condition for the first time. There are deep gashes on her chest. I inspect the wound and decipher the source. She must have been attacked by a feline species. From the blood stains on her tusks and muzzle, I presume she proved the temporary victor.

The master processor has not yet returned, so I decide to determine which creature will be third. My instincts speak to me more naturally this time. Another heartbeat beckons me, more quietly than the boar but louder than the rest. It's one of the pheasants. I sense the cause of her pain. Poison courses through her veins. She has been bitten by a snake.

Before I can consider it further, the steel door opens, and the master processor returns. Even behind his mask, it's evident his impression of me has changed. He no longer regards me with questioning and wonder. He has accepted me in this role, at least for now.

"Madam Providior, have you determined the next creature we must process? Tell me now so we may set to it at once."

"The boar is next, Master Processor."

"*Sir Theo.* You have no cause to regard me by title. I am no master of yours, Madam Providior. What is her condition?"

By his words, I instantly understand the relationship between a master processor and providior as I never before have. *He* is here to assist *me.*

"Sir Theo, the boar has been attacked by some smaller predator, perhaps a feline. Though the boar proved the likely victor in the battle, her injury remains fatal."

His eyes blink behind the mask as he inspects her chest. "Yes, Madam Providior. It is so."

"Before we proceed, Master Processor—"

"Sir Theo—I beg your pardon. Do continue."

"I feel it prudent to inform you of the creature whose condition is next of import."

He says nothing and leans in closer as if I'm about to confide a great secret. "It is one of the pheasants. Though be informed her affliction is snake venom."

"Ah, I see. You learn independently, Madam Providior. The creature is not fit for consumption. So, let us process first the boar, then the pheasant."

"Yes, Master Processor."

He stares at me for a few beats, then issues a cough which I know isn't genuine. I forgot to address him by name.

I nod again, waiting for him to say what I must do. Then I realize I already know. I allow myself to relax. When I feel the sensation of warm and cold returning to my palms, I know it's time.

It is time for me to be who I am.

17

I lean against a wall in a place I know well, the market section of the Harvesting Center. I stand here, oblivious to those perusing the selection of meats and pelts.

I hold up my hands and study my palms. In the artificial light, they look the same, but I know they're changed. Soon my parentes will know what I did, not because I tell them. I'm certain the master processor will.

I peer into the darkness beyond the glass barrier. Lamps now illuminate the Colony Plaza. Encircling the stone ground are brick structures of various heights. They contain merchant centers of devices, garments, foot gear, and zephyrs. The Harvesting Center structure is the grandest of them all.

It is *dies Confucius,* and the plaza is bustling with the usual traffic. I notice two of Jhonis's comrades, Viktor and Yon. I conceal myself behind a display of buffalo hide. I have no desire for them to see me. I'm too exhausted to engage.

A voice beckons me. I offer a weary smile of relief. The master processor has come at last. He appears nervous.

"Madam—*femella.*"

"Yes, Master Processor." I don't call him Sir Theo like I have the past few hours. There are others near, so I address him by title. It feels proper. Though he doesn't correct me, he furls his brows and blinks as if he's uncomfortable with it.

"Come close, femella. There is something I need to impart."

"Yes, Master Processor?"

"Firstly, I appreciate your willingness to wait. I hope I did not keep you too long in my duty with the harvester."

"Not at all."

"Very well. I understand you must be in want of rest after these past hours. Ergo, I shall not keep you from it. I only wish to impart the most prudent of sentiments."

I feel his breath on my ear as his whisper rises to a shallow bark of insistence. "You must tell no one what occurred here this day as none would believe it."

"I understand. Besides, one would regard me as mad if I ever did."

He hints at a relieved smile and bows, and I respond in

kind. He turns and leaves, greeting patrons as he passes them with his usual joviality.

I peer through the barrier to survey the scene. I no longer see Yon and Viktor. I wave my hand in front of the panel to my right and wait for the barrier to retract.

The somber notes of a piano sonata fill the evening air. I lumber down the stone steps, feeling myself succumbing to the mood of the music. I long for the coziness of my pod. Nourishment can wait till morn. All I want is to sleep.

When I reach the base of the steps, the sound of raucous voices on the perimeter breaks the serenity of the music. I labor to raise my head. When I do, I regret it.

It's Jhonis and seven of his comrades including Viktor, Yon, and Diamond. They all ride either horseback or zephyrs. As usual, Diamond accompanies Jhonis in his. I notice they carry wilderness sleep gear. It occurs to me I know why. Last week, I heard them making plans to spend this night on the Annex. There's going to be a total solar eclipse in the morn.

Rafe was supposed to come for me at dawn, and we were going to observe it on the Tower. Perhaps I'll go alone. The consideration is lost when a word creeps into my consciousness.

"Sape!"

Jhonis hisses it, and I'm in no mood. Apparently, he's decided my warning means nothing when his numbers are great, and I stand alone.

"How dare you ignore my beckoning, Sape. Come this instant. Obey like the good pet you are. I require an audience of you."

My flesh warms as I teeter on anger. I ball my hands into fists when something surprising happens.

"Jhonis," Diamond says in her usual manner of exaggerated boredom. "I do believe you are behaving a bit like a feline stalking his prey. Look at how pathetic and ragged her appearance is. Would you not gain more pleasure when her countenance is replenished? As for now, we all wish to proceed with our plans."

"Come now, Diamond. Our plans have been enhanced. I desire to have an audience with Sape, so please do not deny me the entertainment."

I look around at the faces staring back at me. Half seem to be in accord with Diamond. The other half meet my gaze with looks of abhorrence.

In the lamp-lit night, I watch as Jhonis's eyes narrow. I've never seen them this sinister.

"You have no words for me, Sape? How can swine imitate such mastery of self-control? I give you credit to that end, but I will prove it only extends so far."

He leaps from his craft and takes a few attempts at menacing steps. I find my feet meeting him until less than a meter separates us. His eyes flicker in confusion. This isn't what he expects from me. I'm certain he thinks I should cower.

The whites of his eyes redden. His rage is obvious. I feel pity. He's nothing to me. He's a bully. I find strength in this weakness.

I peer into his pitiful gray eyes and feel the weight of his heaving breath. "You wish for me to exchange words with you? Well, in this case, young Jhonis, allow me to express this. Your antics have grown stale. They bore me in fact. *You* bore me."

"How can swine filth ever bore? Do you feel out of sorts from your pile of mud?"

"I assure you, I feel most at ease where I stand. Now, in reference to you complimenting my ease of self-control, it is something no being could say of you. I wish you could see your face in this moment."

His fleeting grimace transforms into a wicked smile. In the ambience of the baroque music, his expression is absurd.

"I merely speak the language of your beastly ignorance. I reduce myself so your simple mind will comprehend me."

"You execute it so eloquently, I am convinced it is your true nature. Now, leave me in peace. I have better ways to spend this night than to waste another moment in your company. You're pathetic. I can't even call you vile, since you're too feeble of mind to warrant such a label of strength."

His lips quiver. Mine retract in a grin. His hands ball into fists. Mine are relaxed and steady.

He takes a step closer to me. I can feel and smell each

wave of his breath. It carries the scent of tart rosemary nectar. He's been imbibing.

"You pithy, little gutter rodent." His voice slithers with malice. With each syllable he utters, I find him more ridiculous. He lowers his voice so only I can hear his next words. "I will spend each day of my life ensuring you suffer in your miserable, worthless existence, *Sape*. I will make it my duty to ensure you only know despair."

"If you mean to unhinge me, young Jhonis, you will need to be more convincing. Allow me to demonstrate. You are a surface-crawling, poisonless bug who means to frighten a wolf. Mind yourself, Jhonis, for I will trample you beneath my toe without ever knowing you existed."

"You call *me* a bug, you filthy Sape?" he screams. He leans closer. Our noses touch. I stare into his blazing eyes. I narrow mine and wink. He growls and opens his mouth to speak. Something to his left causes him to pause. I turn to see a dark form moving with purpose and grace, accompanied by the sound of hooves.

I'm too dazzled to question the black stallion's appearance. As he halts at my side, I say with a lofty air, "It would appear I am saved from walking this night, so I will bid you a good eve, Jhonis. It has not been a pleasure, and I do *not* anticipate the next time we meet."

As I labor to mount my champion, I remember how exhausted I am. I bury my face in his mane and embrace the comfort of his scent. I'm about to direct him when I notice Jhonis moving his lips. He's whispering.

"Buck your passenger, beast. Throw her to the ground and trample her."

My stomach lurches from disgust. He employs his ability for harm. It's an unforgivable violation.

The stallion releases a savage squeal and throws himself onto his hinds. I think he's trying to buck me, but he does something else. He kicks his front legs outward, landing one of them with a resounding blow onto Jhonis's chest.

It happens so fast. I'm frozen in place and in time.

Jhonis falls to the ground, landing on the stone with a helpless thud. I watch from above as he props himself onto his elbows, his eyes bulging with fear. There's nothing I can do but watch the wave of repeated blows of hooves on chest. It doesn't stop until Jhonis holds deathly still.

Shrieks and thudding of feet penetrate the night. Mahogany and green flash before me as Diamond dives to the ground beneath me. The rest of them stare at me with fear, disgust, and rage.

"Your foul Sape scent caused the black stallion to trample our comrade!" Grindol screeches.

Terror, fear, and confusion saturate my blood. He blames me when Jhonis uttered the attack.

Yon accuses me next. His lemon-colored hair whips about his deep-brown face as he screams in rage. "Your Sape blood has tainted this creature. Your filth made him attack."

I bury my face in the black mane. It feels slick against my face from my tears. "Take me from this place, Black Stallion. Run fast and fierce."

He carries me into the darkness, away from the rich music and crowd now gathering at the scene. I focus on the sound of his breath, my terror increasing with each stride. I close my eyes and beg him to run faster.

18

My tears have dried. I have no more to give. I lie on the back of the graceful creature in a crumble of remorse. His honor is destroyed, and it's because of me. He came to my aid and will now suffer the mistrust of everyone in our colony. It won't matter to them that Jhonis caused it. The black stallion will be exiled, forced from his territory.

Someone will whisper to him. They'll implore him to leave and never return. The person must be me. I owe it to him. He was protecting me instead of heeding a hateful summons.

Guilt and fear flood my soul, my mind—every bit of me. I hope Jhonis is okay. Never did I wish him harm. Never did I want him dead.

When our pace slows to a trot, I'm lulled by his gentle sway. I don't know how long we've been riding or what direction we travel. It's too dark, and we're under the thick cover of trees.

We ride for kilometers when we reach the edge of the forest. I look to the stars and discover we've travelled far north. It's as if he knows his fate.

The lightning farms are near. I wonder why he came here, so close to the farms he must—by nature—fear. I decide it's time to dismount, ignoring the question of how I'll return.

I shiver from the cold and my task. I have no choice.

I whisper.

"Salvē, Black Stallion. Thank you for your service this night, but now you must go and never return. Though you are blameless, all who know of this night will fear you. You are too noble to suffer it. You must find a new place to roam where none have ever before seen you…where I might never again see you. Set your course to the far West or East, to the safety of the Wild."

I pause, stroking his neck and feeling his breath on my face. "As you depart, know I regret these utterances upon your graceful soul. It is not what I wish, but it is necessary. Farewell, Black Stallion. I hope to be honored by seeing you again someday in some distant colony. Until then, I wish you an auspicious journey. Now you must go."

I conclude my summons and await his reaction. What he does fills me with warmth. He places his muzzle to my forehead and licks me. Never before has he done such a thing. He lowers his head and presses it to my palm. I stroke his face. He makes a gentle nicker. Usually it means hello. On this night, he is saying farewell.

I offer a few pats on his neck and say, "Until next we meet."

As he turns from me and trots westward, my throat tightens, and my eyes fill with tears. I long for him to remain, but I know he can't. I watch as he disappears into the night. I listen for the sound of his hooves until it fades to silence.

I stand alone in the darkness with only the light of my device to illuminate the night. My parentes don't have a zephyr, so contacting my mater to fetch me will do no good. And I would rather walk than contact Rafe for help.

My parentes are probably wondering where I am. I've been gone all day. I decide to contact them after I find a horse to ride.

I shine my light the direction we came. It's going to be a long walk, and I have no desire to begin. I direct my light to the North, curiosity compelling me to see a place I've never been.

I direct my feet forward and stop when the natural terrain abruptly ends. I shine my light on the ground and see an expanse of concrete.

The farther I walk, the more I feel a pulsing of energy. I should stop. I should turn and go south. But all that's waiting for me in my colony are explanations and grief. So I keep walking toward the fields.

The energy grows stronger with each step. Dark, massive forms appear, reaching several kilometers to the sky. They're rows of concrete and metal towers, and they're daunting in the darkness. Interspersed among them are long and narrow concrete pools of water.

Only an aerisma is allowed in a lightning farm. They channel lightning in these fields, harvesting and storing it by combining their ability, lasers, and magnetic technology. This one must be where all the colonies in this sector of the province receive electrical power. There's no impending storm, so no aerisma is here to patrol the laser towers or monitor data.

The energy in this place causes my teeth to tingle and the hairs on my flesh to stand on end. I almost feel dazed. As I roam amidst the concrete and metal giants, I feel tiny.

I've wandered so far into the field that I'm disoriented. I wave my light in search of the southern end. I look to the stars, but the tower nearest me obstructs my view. I shift several paces to the left, and my heart flutters when my foot extends downward instead of landing on solid ground.

I can't stop my momentum. My leg scrapes the rough surface as my arms flail for balance. My throat seizes in horror when I feel my foot sinking in water. My body spasms. I can't move as I watch the towers toppling to their sides. I'm falling.

My brain commands me to hold my breath. I land with a

splash into the icy water. I can't move my limbs to swim to safety. I sink to the depths until I land on the concrete floor of the pool. Twice I'm drowning, only now there's no one here to save me.

My eyes seek the surface, but my body does not comply. The stars shimmer against the black sky. It's the last thing I'll see.

My lungs start to burn.

A dark figure circles the stars. It moves swiftly…*down-ward.* It's directly above me—a dark, winged form.

I can't hold my breath any longer. Water floods my mouth, devouring me as the electric currents paralyze me.

Something callous and strong wraps itself around me. It hoists me upward until I burst through the watery grave.

A flood of oxygen embraces me as the weight of the water tumbles to the concrete. I'm caged in a grip as solid as iron. My weightless body climbs to the sky to mingle with the stars.

I'm not dead. The cold wind tells me I'm alive. I smell the scent of winged flesh. I'm cradled in the talon of the master eagle.

My head rolls to the side. I can see the pools below, dark and menacing, and thirsting for my death.

A wave of vomit spills from my mouth, releasing in a spray on the wind. Through watery eyes, images appear before me. Energy surrounds me, its electric limbs longing to trap me in their embrace.

The sensation is too great. The sting of tears is too great. I close my eyes. My body is limp. I'm floating on the wind.

19

The mighty talon no longer envelops me when I open my eyes. Instead I feel the hardness of concrete beneath me. The sound of panting hovers at my ear. Something slick strokes my cheek. I blink, and a short, wet snout nudges my face in response.

Hints of light inform me it's early morn. As I become more aware, I realize I'm lying on the bench, under the Weeping Willow of my grounds. The master eagle delivered me to this spot. I must have whispered to him to bring me here.

The last thing I remember is floating on the onyx sky, the twinkling stars and moon lighting our way.

I should have died last night, but the master eagle rescued

me. How could he have even known I was there?

Twice in one night two great creatures came to my aid. The master eagle risked his life. The black stallion sacrificed his grace.

My stomach plummets at the thought of him, and the memories of the trampling bombard me. Jhonis may be dead.

A squat, white and brown face eclipses my view and licks me again. It's a male canine, a descendent of the ancient pit bull. His tongue dangles from his panting mouth, and he looks at me with play in his eyes. I roll to my side and extend a hand to stroke his head.

"Salvē, Canine. Thank you for bringing me to consciousness."

He pants and wines and licks me again.

"I would love to pass this time with you, but there is something I must do. Good day, Canine, and be cautious of the wolves as I know you will be."

He releases a playful bark before plodding away, his muscular hind swaying in his trot. I wonder where his pack must be. It's not safe for him to be alone when the wolves roam this quadrant of forest. As if to allay my concern, he howls. In the distance I hear the barks and howls of other canines, and I know he'll be met with safe travels.

I seek the sun behind a narrow clearing of trees, but it's still below the horizon. I push myself off the bench, and the world spins and my head feels light. I press my hands to my forehead, waiting for it to pass.

The energy feels like it still surges within me, making me feel strange and unlike myself. Flashes of thought enter my mind and leave before I can process it all. Images also appear. They're horrific. My eyes squeeze shut as if the act will make them fade.

I become aware of how disjointed I feel. The pool's affects remind me of the terrifying conclusion to an emotionally erratic day.

It's too early for my parentes to be awake. Since neither attempted to contact me last night, they probably believe I returned without alerting them of my presence.

I cross my grounds on legs weak with hunger and trauma. When I'm a few meters from the veranda steps, I hear voices in the culina. Not only are my parentes awake, they're not alone. The third voice is one I have no desire to hear. It belongs to Rafe. Suddenly it occurs to me why he's here. He must have come to honor our plan of viewing the eclipse, as if nothing has changed between us.

I can't bring myself to see him. I crouch at the base of the steps, concealing myself from view, waiting for my pater to tell him to leave.

Their voices are muffled through the barrier, but I can still understand their words.

"Do not bid me to calm myself, Sapphire. We may not be so fortunate the next time she performs such an act. How long before someone discovers what she has done? When it becomes known, the colony will demand answers. How long are we to tolerate this? I was forced to assume airs of ignorance in the presence of Sir William."

"Sir Roman, perhaps you might consider this from her perspective. She feels alone."

After everything I said to him, Rafe still defends me. My irritation from his presence wanes in the timbre of his voice.

"Do not presume to understand her more than we do. Need I remind you, you are her appointed comrade. *We* are her *parentes.*"

"Roman!"

Appointed comrade?

"Tend to your manners, Roman. I demand it."

The room falls to silence until a guttural sigh interrupts it. "Do pardon my impropriety. I lose myself in worry. This situation in which we find ourselves…First, it was the master eagle. Now it is the preternatural events at the Tank. I shudder to ask, yet I must. Rafe, is there something else which she might have confessed to you alone?"

"Sir Roman, whether there is or is not, by posing such a question, you violate the privilege of confidence between comrades."

"I do not believe there is anything for him to confide, when Rayne has already confessed all."

"So, are we simply to await the next incident?"

"I suppose it is all we can do."

"This is madness!"

"Reduce your volume, Roman."

My pater groans. "I might be able to accomplish the task in his absence. Ergo, Sir Rafe, I believe it is time for you to leave. You should not even be here at this hour. Why have you come?"

"Roman, you forget yourself again. He has come to collect Rayne to view the eclipse. This you already know."

"You will pardon my failure to recall it. Actually, there is something I *do* recall. Sapphire, did you not say Rayne has broken ties with him?"

"Sir Roman, I came hoping she might forgive me."

"You may hope as much as you wish *after* you leave this domus, without her."

"You lose your manners, Roman."

"In this moment, I care not of manners. What are we to do? What next we will be *compelled* to do? Soon we will have no choice but to confess to the Board and await whatever actions they see fit."

"Roman, lower your voice."

After a pause, my pater resumes speaking, but I can no longer decipher his words. I hold my breath as if it'll help me hear him. I have to get closer. I place my foot on the first step, and I cringe.

Rafe flinches and is the first to turn in my direction. I

know he sees me. My mater turns next. She opens her mouth to speak, but my pater does first.

"Rayne! How long have you been present? Why are you not in your chamber? What have you heard?"

My face grows hot. It is I who should be demanding why they were discussing me in my absence. I want to scream, but instead, I climb the steps. I avoid their worried stares as I grab a peach from the fruit basin and march to the salon, my body threatening to collapse.

I devour the peach as I hear footsteps approach. I decide I don't want to hear anything they have to say right now. It's too much. I want to leave.

My pater peeks into the salon, and I go to him. My hand lifts on its own, my palm facing down.

He raises his hand, expecting that I mean to give him something. I do.

I place the slimy pit in his hand as I walk past him to leave. Before I step into the brisk air in search of the sun, I hear him gag. Then he calls my name.

20

Once again, I'm a jumble of thoughts and emotions. Anything more and I'll crumble from the weight of it all. I need to regroup. I go where I can gaze at the sky and try not to think. I seek the plains on foot.

Looming over everything are the words, *appointed comrade*. I try to convince myself my pater carelessly spoke.

What's even more daunting is all these abilities coursing through me. I'll be compelled to race from one duty to the next. I'll never have rest.

How can I consider all this a gift? I know it's supposed to be, but it doesn't feel like it. It feels like a curse. I wish it was last week, and the only ability I ever discovered was the first.

Without it, the master eagle never would have come for me, and I would be dead.

Though I try to quiet them, my thoughts continue in a maddening swirl. Never before have I experienced the fullness of the word, overwhelmed. I need to forget what is and what might be, if only for a day.

When I arrive at the eastern edge of the forest, the sun is well above the horizon. I activate my ocular shield and find a place in the wild grass. I lie down and nestle in its embrace. Tiny insects draw to my heat and crawl up my weary body. I brush one from my face and prop my head on my arms.

I look to the sky. The moon eclipses the sun by nearly half. I activate the recording function of my device. I tap my fingers again to enlarge the field, imagining I can touch the moon.

As I lie here in solitude, my emotions threaten to make me burst. I know where I have to go, but I can't seem to force myself to move.

I try not to replay the incident in my mind, but I do. A slight breeze brushes my face. My lids grow heavy, and I allow them. I need the peace of sleep.

A scene appears before me. I must be dreaming, because I know I'm still lying in the plains. It's night in the plaza. Jhonis appears from thin air, lying on the ground beneath me. Something is trampling him, but it's not the black stallion's hooves. It's me.

My legs don't move, but I watch as his chest caves with each blow until he lies lifeless on the ground. Blood trickles from his mouth and pools on his neck. The flow doesn't stop until all hope of life is lost.

When I realize what I've done, I open my mouth to scream. No sound emits from my throat. My jaw clenches, my muscles become tense, and somehow I force myself awake.

My forehead is wet with my sweat. My body shakes, and I blink to erase the images. I focus on the sky and remind myself it was just a dream.

Yet what happened is real.

The light of the evening sky blankets me. The moon no longer eclipses the sun. The infinite stars are beginning to appear, like shimmering grains on a rich, midnight-blue satiny fabric. I sit upright, confused by this passage of time. I've been asleep for several hours.

A creepy feeling plagues me. My body is crawling with insects. They're on my face and in my hair. I jump to my feet and brush them off in a crazed rush. I tousle my hair and scratch at my scalp. I activate the light on my device and sweep it across my body until I'm certain no insect remains.

My breathing finally steadies. I look around me. I'm still alone. It's time for me to leave. I can no longer justify avoiding it. I have to learn if Jhonis is okay.

I go to the most likely place where I might find news of his condition. People will be at the plaza wanting to know precisely where and how the incident occurred. Though I worry how they'll react to my presence, I have no choice.

As I walk, hunger anchors my body. My stomach is nauseous from the lack of fuel. I can't continue like this, and I wonder if my conscience wishes me to starve to death.

I stumble to the plaza, my chest heaving from exhaustion. The pit of my empty stomach lurches to meet my throat. I swallow the acidic liquid and grimace at the taste.

As the usual baroque music saturates the evening air, I'm haunted by the memories. The anticipation makes it worse. I force my feet forward, my footfall producing a soft thud as I walk across the earthen stone.

The plaza is quiet tonight. Peculiarly quiet. The lights in the markets are all extinguished. No one is present. There are only creatures here: a pack of canines sniffing about the Harvesting Center for scraps they know will never come; a few horses watering at the brook; and some birds nestling in the trees for the night. The sonorous melody and voices of the creatures adds to the vibe of an eerie serenade.

My feet lead me toward the tram terminal on the opposite end of the plaza. I enter the ascensus for the short lift to the platform. The moment I exit, I sink to the surface and lean against the glass wall. The next tram will arrive in eleven minutes. I have never longed for it as much as I do now.

Something in the distance draws my attention, in a narrow clearing of trees. I see unmistakable tram lights travelling west. There's no performance, so it shouldn't be in service.

A nagging sensation tells me the answer is obvious. I know where everyone is. They've gathered in the amphitheater to discuss the horrific event. Only such a thing as the trampling would cause them to convene there.

It's our place of meeting for major assemblies. They rarely occur. Twice in my life my parentes have gone there for some meeting of which I was never apprised. This is the third time, and it's about me.

I wait, weak from hunger, until the tram arrives. I force myself to my feet and board it. For the first time, I ride it solo. I seek my usual place in the front, feeling eerily alone.

The barriers seal, and the tram propels forward in its smooth glide. I listen to the whoosh of air. It's too loud. There's no murmur of voices to silence it.

By the time the tram ascends to its height above the trees, the sky is completely dark. I wish I boarded earlier to witness the setting sun shooting its brilliant, blood-orange rays beyond the Great Mountains. My heart flutters at the thought of the color. It makes me think of Rafe. I force all thoughts of him from my mind. I focus on the splendor of darkness and the sparkling sky.

I allow my imagination to roam as it always does on the tram. I'm hurtling through space, travelling in the opposite direction of the spinning Earth. I imagine myself in a ship, floating amongst the stars, admiring the lights of Earth from a great distance.

Yet, those lights draw nearer and brighter. They're not stars. They're the lights in the amphitheater.

As the tram slows in its approach, my breath seizes. My knees collapse, forcing me to crouch below the glass. The tram stops. I have several seconds to decide whether I'll be brave or cower on the floor.

I must face them. I must disembark.

The tram signals its departure as I go to the nearest rope ladder. I propel myself over the edge, relieved to be shielded in darkness.

I climb to the ground, my balmy hands betraying my fear of what I know I'll discover: Jhonis is dead, and my colony blames me for it.

I take the cover behind the rock wall as I descend the steps. I allow myself to believe the amphitheater is vacant. But the farther I go, the sound of voices extinguishes my hope.

The murmurs transition to distinguishable male and female inflections. I peek around the wall, straining to hear any discernible word or sentiment. Nearly half my colony is here.

The sea of multicolored heads makes the scene look beautiful. Brightly dyed shades of color mingle with natural browns, blonds, and grays. I find myself searching for blood-orange.

Everyone is seated. I lean a bit farther around the wall and see the bright-green streaks which belong only to Diamond. She sits in the center of them all.

Next to her are a male and female around the age of my parentes. The male has a short, blond beard and a natural-blond head of hair. The female is thin and delicate with wide, gray eyes. Her light-brown hair is cut short to reveal the full length of her neck. They're Jhonis's parentes, and the sight of their distress makes me fear the worst.

A row of Conifers lines the steps. I creep around the wall to seek cover behind the nearest one. It's a mistake.

The talking ceases, and the silence startles me like a splash of cold wind. I hold my breath as if it'll make me invisible.

All eyes are on me, stunned and unwelcoming. I approach them humbly, losing confidence with each step. All of them look at me like I'm a thing called disease.

When a masculine voice breaks the awkward silence, I regret my decision to come. "How dare you present yourself in our midst after what you have done!" It's Grindol. Though he stands several meters from me, I can clearly see the spit in his eyes. A murmur of assent echoes throughout the vast space. I don't know what to say, so I remain silent.

"Perhaps her arrival is fortuitous. Now we may discuss the terms of her banishment," a female voice declares. Another wave of accord rolls through the crowd. I don't dare to look for my parentes to see if they agree.

"You hear that, Sape?" Grindol hisses. "We all wish for your banishment. It was your tainted essence which incited that noble creature to inflict severe injury."

Inflict severe injury.

"He lives? Jhonis *lives?*"

"It is of no concern to you," another voice yells from deeper in the crowd. It belongs to a magister at Institute, Magister Biboye. He leads my favorite discussion.

My heart sinks at the declaration from another male voice. "None have requested your presence in this place. You have committed enough heinous acts. You have fouled a beast of the Earth. You have soiled his soul and incited him to attack a human being. None wish to look upon you after what you have done. Depart at once."

My body weakens with sorrow. The words are like a dagger to my heart. They're words from a voice I know well.

"Please, Pater. I beg of you. All of you. I am not at fault for the horrific accident. It is Jhonis who caused it. Now, I beg of you to tell me his condition so my heart may know whether to mourn or to rejoice with you."

"We wish you to do neither!" a female yells.

"You dare spit lies in our faces to falsely vindicate yourself?" Grindol growls. "How dare you speak ill of a victim when he cannot himself attest to what occurred. We should expect no more from you. We all know the truth of your tainted DNA. Your *Sape* genes."

The utter disregard of propriety stuns me as all of them murmur in accord. I have to defend myself, because no one here will.

"Grindol, you witnessed it yourself. You know what Jhonis whispered to the black stallion. Denying it will serve nothing. *I do not speak lies.* Regardless, I am not here in defense of myself. I have only come to learn of his condition. I implore you—all of you—to behave with grace in this moment. Am I not a member of this colony still?"

"You are *not* one of us. You are a being which should not even exist. You are an abomination, and we all wish for you to leave this colony for good."

When Grindol says nothing more, another wave of murmurs floods the pit of the amphitheater. They all stare at me. I search their faces for any hints of empathy, but only bitterness greets me.

The longer I meet their stares, the more desperate I become. "I have come in good will to inquire as to the health of a human life, yet none of you will behave in turn by giving me an account of his status. *No one,*" I say with a fierceness which my parentes must know is directed at them.

"You are not deserving of propriety, *Sape.*" Murmurs shift to a simmering hiss. They're all in alignment with Grindol.

An electric pulse surges through me. I tighten my hands into fists to quiet the sensation. It doesn't work. It grows stronger with each dismal beat of my heart. I battle to confine it. I force my hands to spread in submissive protest.

"Please. Will none here inform me of his condition?"

No one speaks. Something else happens which is worse. An arm slowly raises to the sky, the fingers spread wide, the palm flat. More arms lift and hands position themselves, then another and another until all arms are extended. All hands are raised.

By this act, they display their desire to speak against me. It's a silent vote, a visual cue that they're all in accord, and I stand alone against them.

Only one hand breaks my heart: my pater's. For the second time, he acts against me. He's showing me he doesn't love me. Now I wonder if he ever has.

But next to him is hope. My mater holds her hands firmly in her lap. I concentrate on this.

A voice speaks, but I don't heed the words. I know it belongs to Grindol. I know his words are hateful. Then another voice speaks, and another. This isn't supposed to happen. They're not supposed to speak at once against one person. What they do now is something abhorrent. They're all united to bully me. They lower their moral standards to do so. There's no doubt how much they despise me.

The energy within me surges again. It's almost electric as it pulses in my hands and into my fingertips.

The voices are more animated. Their words overlap with volume and intensity. This is wrong. They shouldn't be doing this. I don't deserve this.

My palms contract. My fingers extend toward them.

The pulsing of energy is hot. No, it is *cold.* Deathly cold. The sensation causes me to retract my arms. My chest heaves. It doesn't feel right. I need to stop this. I need to *release* this.

They shout at me now. They taunt me. They *hate* me. All except my mater. Her head is lowered. I wish she would look at me. I need her to look at me. I need her to help me calm this rage.

The voices are too loud. I feel a scream rising in my throat. I must silence them all.

My arms writhe with an electric force. I need to push it away so I no longer feel it. A scream forces its way through my mouth as I thrust my arms forward, my hands held out to tell them all to stop.

My scream echoes in my ears as my eyes burn with a fury I've never known. The force of it sends me reeling, and I soar through the air.

The moment my back crashes onto the sharp edge of a step, I see them all. They all move en masse, in a pace which seems slower than real time. Their bodies fall backward, like blades of wild grass blowing in the wind. They all collapse, their faces slack, their bodies limp.

I struggle for breath to scream, but each inhale ushers a writhing pain. My head lolls to the ground, and all I see are the stars in the sky.

I ignore the pain in my body as I turn my head toward them all. They lie motionless on the steps. I moan and shriek and scream as I gaze into the depths of what I've done. I killed my parentes. I killed them all.

The rumors about me are kind. They never called me evil, but now I know that I am.

21

I am limp. Weightless. I open my eyes to see Rafe carrying me. He wasn't in the amphitheater when I slayed half my colony. Otherwise, he would be dead, too.

It's so vivid, like it's happening all over again, that I scream.

"Rayne…you must calm yourself or I will drop you."

His voice is gentle and soothing, like he doesn't know about the massacre. But he was there, or I wouldn't be with him now. He knows what I did.

"What have I done? What have I *done?*"

"Focus on remaining calm, Rayne. Just a bit farther to your villa."

"How can I rest after—" I realize he's still carrying me like an infant, and suddenly I feel foolish. I lurch from his grip and throw myself onto feeble legs.

"What are you doing?"

"How can you be so nonchalant after what I have done? I am wicked."

"Wicked? I think you exaggerate."

I stare at him, my head aching with confusion. The images haunt me. I killed them all with some hellish force. I watched as they all collapsed to their deaths. I press my fingers to my temples to erase the memory.

"Rayne, you will feel better once you lie down."

"I will *never* feel better."

The agony hardens in my gut and reminds me how weak I am from hunger. I feel my knees slackening and my body sinking. Rafe catches me and hoists me in his arms. Weakness overwhelms my horror and embarrassment.

Then blackness surrounds me.

When I open my eyes, I'm lying on a lounge in my salon. When I see my pater's holodigit on the table, I remember. They're all dead, and I killed them.

I weep.

I hear the sound of pouring water in the culina. Like the children and elders, Rafe survived whatever evil it was when I employed some new gift of the Luminescence. I've left the children and elders without their familiae. The thought crushes my soul, and I wish I could drown myself in tears.

I wish I drowned. Diamond never should've saved me. The master eagle never should've risked his life for me. If I was dead, they would all still be alive.

"Rayne."

Rafe stands over me, holding a vessel of water. I wipe the tears from my eyes, refusing to accept it. "Water is the giver of life, and I am undeserving of it after what I have done. Leave me, and tend to the elders and children who are grieving in this hour."

"Grieving? Rayne, please drink this. I do not believe you are well."

"How can I be well when I have caused them all such great sorrow? When the morn comes, the children will wake to suffer the deepest essence of the word."

"To what sorrow will they awake?"

I stare at him, confused by his lack of sympathetic decency. He speaks again before I can rebuke him.

"You are weak, Rayne, confused, whether from lack of sustenance or shock."

"I have *killed*, Rafe. I cannot be here. Not in this domus. Not in this colony."

I sit up, ignoring the nauseous sensation which threatens to send me toppling to my side. I plant my feet on the ground and stand, wondering where I'll go, what I'll do, and how I'll bear what I've done.

"Rayne…Jhonis *lives*. Though he is in dire health, he still lives. The medica are doing all they can for him. But know this. Whether he lives or dies, I know it was not you who caused it. I know it was he who set that creature against you." He stares at me, his eyes tender and wet with compassion.

I shake my head, indifferent to his belief in my innocence. It now seems miniscule. Whether Jhonis lives or dies, I will still be the homicida of half my colony.

"How can you act as though it is the most significant thing after what I have done? I know you were there. I know you saw."

"I think you need rest."

"I have slept and lost consciousness enough. How can you react to what I have done with such apathy?" As I say this, I shudder from the images of the dead.

"If you require it so you may rest, I will address it. I was there this night. I remained on the perimeter. I did not wish to be in the presence of so many who spoke ill of you. I only entered the amphitheater when I heard you speaking in your defense. I believed each syllable you uttered. All who hold you at fault are misguided by fear of the unknown. I regret my silence. I should have declared the black stallion should be commended for his defense of you."

"Everyone is dead because of me!"

"*What?* I believe you are on the verge of insanity."

We stare at each other, both confused. Neither of us speaks.

Then I hear approaching footsteps. *Familiar footsteps.* It's the footfall of the dead.

My heart pounds. I'm afraid of what I'll see. I hear voices in the corridor. Familiar voices. They don't belong to ghosts. I don't know how it's possible, but they're here, and they're alive.

"Mater! Pater!"

"Rafe, thank you for escorting her. As for you, Rayne, perhaps it is time for you to retire to your chamber."

When I hear the words falling from my pater's lips, I feel like I'm trapped between dream and consciousness.

I want to run to them, to embrace them. Then I look into his eyes, and I remember what he did. So I sit here, confused, relieved, and brimming with hurt.

"Roman, take care your fatigue does not spike your tongue."

My flesh tingles from my mater's admonishing words. They are *here*—standing, breathing, and speaking.

"Dear Rayne, you look terribly peakish. When was the last time you had sustenance?"

"Mater, how are you here? How—"

"*Twice* you have brought great shame upon us, Rayne."

"Roman! Silence your tongue lest I insist you depart at once."

"You chastise *me?* Did you not witness what she did? Now all in this colony know the aberrations of which she alone is capable."

"Let them speak ill as they have always done. It should bear no weight on our relations with our filia."

"Filia? Must I remind you, she is not our—"

"Watch yourself, Roman, lest you find yourself forbidden to return within these walls and forced to sleep among the creatures and insects of night."

I barely hear their exchange. They're all still live? Questions float in my mind which I need to resolve, yet the words don't come. If I didn't kill anyone, are they all unscathed by whatever force caused them to appear lifeless? I press my hands to my temples to stifle the disorientation and light-headedness.

I lower my head and stare at the floor. I must be imagining all this. They're apparitions. If I close my eyes, I'll discover I'm dreaming. When I open them, my parentes will disappear. I'll awake to the reality that they're dead.

"Sir Roman, Lady Sapphire, please. We are troubling Rayne."

I hear the scuffle of someone drawing near. Olive-toned feet with nails painted azure blue appear within my view. My mater wears my favorite color on her toes. I study them, fixating on the rich tone, believing my mind has fabricated them for longing of what is forever lost.

She kneels before me and places her hands on mine, lowering them to my lap. She lightly touches my chin and lifts my face to hers. When I meet her eyes, I know she's no illusion. Apparitions do not weep.

"Dear Rayne, I beg your forgiveness for failing to voice my discord with them all. Also know this. Though his condition is critical, Jhonis still lives. I do not believe for an instant it was the result of anything to do with you. I believe it was his own atrocity and hypocrisy which caused it. I believe he whispered to the noble creature to inflict harm upon *you.* Though not all in this room are in accord with this truth, take comfort that two of us are. You have been wrongly denounced for the acts of another. You are a victim here too, and all in this domus will regard you as such or else their presence will no longer be welcome."

Her final words strike with a force I've never before heard her utter. They're an ultimatum to my pater—if I can ever again regard him as such.

Yet, I find myself fixating on one thing. "How are you alive? How is it you have gone from a sea of corpses to walking and speaking with no evidence of what I did?"

I search my mater's eyes for anything to explain it. I look to my pater, thinking he'll delight in recounting my heinous crimes, yet he remains silent. He doesn't even look at me.

"Dear Rayne," my mater begins, her voice gentle and sympathetic, "your lack of sustenance has caused you to imagine something worse than actually was. You inflicted no harm beyond minor scrapes from the impact of meeting the ground unwittingly."

"How? I watched as it occurred. You were all dead. Of that I am certain…was certain."

My mater looks to Rafe, whose face is filled with pity. "Rayne," he says, taking a step toward me. He moves as though he wishes to sit beside me, then changes his mind, brushing his hair to occupy his hands. "You harmed no one. We were all met with some electric, magnetic jolt. All we suffered was a momentary lapse of consciousness. You, however, remained unconscious for the greater part of an hour."

"I thought you were all dead," I whisper, my throat dry and my voice croaking through tears.

"As you can see, it is not the case." Rafe speaks with such compassion that I finally believe him.

"What was it then? How did I do it? There is no ability which can cause such a thing."

I stare at my hands, almost afraid of them. I recall what it felt like. It was like my hands were charged with an electromagnetic pulse. It was like I was in the energy pool again. Then I understand. Through the Luminescence, I am a magnos, and the energy pool must have made it dangerous.

"Roman, you will inform her of our conclusions."

My pater feigns a cough, avoiding my stare. He clears his throat and speaks as if the act causes him great pain. "After lengthy discussion as to the physics behind what you have done, it is the conclusion that you have always possessed the dormant ability of magnos. It is now believed that your mater and I merely failed at diligently exploring all possibilities. All have agreed the reason this ability is so strong is you have only now just deployed it. It is the culmination of years of stored energy which you fully unleashed this night."

When he finishes, he stares at the ground, refusing to look at me.

"You should know, Rayne, it was your pater who suggested this notion," my mater says.

"You are fortunate I possess quick wit, Rayne. Otherwise all would be known, and I would have been met with even more disgrace. Though none this night were harmed in body, I cannot speak to their minds, so quick they were to accept such an explanation. Regardless, everyone still holds you accountable for the harm inflicted upon Jhonis. Whether the colony believes you have always possessed an ability does nothing to alter their justified opinion of you. You have made yourself a persona non grata with your actions toward Jhonis and to us all this night. You are fortunate none beyond us three know the full truth. Now I must suffer the disgrace that I share my domus with an abomination."

My mouth bursts open from a flood of tears. I feel my mater's arms wrapping around me. I hear the fierce rumbling of her voice as she spits animosity toward my pater.

"Roman, with these words, you have disgraced yourself. Another word from your lips, and I will curse the day I pledged my life to yours. Rest soundly this night, Roman, for you will not do so in *my* chamber."

"I do say, Sir Roman, you have the uncanny ability to make yourself despised by those who are pure enough to love you. You are a wretched man who has lost the privilege of being a pater."

"You will silence your insubordinate tongue and leave at once!"

"I will remain until either Lady Sapphire or Rayne bids me to leave."

"Be quiet!" I shriek. I push myself to my feet, my head pounding, my body teetering on convulsions. "I am on the verge of insanity. Any more of this and I will burst. Unless, however, you prefer I alleviate your disgrace by my death, *Sir Roman.*"

I force my quivering legs to carry me to my chamber. I collapse onto my pod, and there's only one thing which comforts me enough to seek sleep. Whatever the new day will bring, I know I'm not a slayer of humanity.

22

As the light of morn brightens my chamber, my dream still haunts me. The images appear before me as clearly as if I'm still asleep. It's like the dream I had in the plains, but this one is more horrific. The pooling blood is on my hands, wet, thick, and warm. Even now that I'm awake, it still feels so real. I stare at my hands, horrified the blood will reappear.

This dream will return to me each time I sleep until I do what my conscience bids me. I have to see Jhonis with my own eyes.

A hunger pang strikes me. It's been 48 hours since I ate a proper meal. Or less? I can no longer tell.

Starvation has caused me to hallucinate the savory scent of

nourishment floating on the air. The aroma is so enticing that I feel myself bewitched. It lures me to turn my head.

Sitting on my table is a savory dish and vessel of liquid. There's enough for two. Next to the plate of food is a note painted in lilac on a writing tablet:

Do forgive me for my invasion of your privacy. I wanted to ensure you received proper nourishment this day. Please take care not to forego it. You may remain in your chamber as long as you wish. I have instructed your pater to remain beyond the walls of this villa until I return. It is dies Nightingale, so I will see you at midday. With love, Mater.

I devour the contents like the ravenous beast everyone thinks I am. I barely taste it. I don't deserve such a luxury. I merely need fuel for what I must do.

It's been nearly a week since my reality has shifted to the chaos it is now. It feels like a lifetime ago. Tomorrow will be *dies Gandhi,* the first day back to Institute after the three-day hiatus. I have no intention of attending anymore.

Yet, there are two I have to see if my horrible dreams will ever stop. One is the victim of his own crime. The other is Diamond. As I ready myself for the day, I believe she'll help me. Though it didn't register at the time, Diamond didn't raise her hand against me last night.

There are two places where I could find her. Most likely, she'll be with Jhonis. I don't dare go to his villa alone. There's a small possibility she'll be at Institute. Only the magisters and apprentices attend today. Diamond is an apprentice, so I decide to go there first.

In order to get there before her duties begin, I have to travel by horse. At this hour, I won't have any issue finding one at the brook in the forest.

I bolt outside and run. My lungs are still fresh when I reach the brook, and I'm not alone. Two magisters are here. I consider waiting for them to leave but decide I can't cower forever. I remind myself that soon this colony will be a distant memory. Until then, I have no choice but to endure their loathing.

I'm a few paces from them when the male notices me. When I offer a smile, he feigns not to notice.

"Good morn, Magister Cruz, Magister Inira."

Magister Inira offers a polite smile as she mounts her horse. Magister Cruz mounts his then turns to me, his lips firmly pressed and his forehead creasing with disdain.

My eyes are locked on his. I can't free myself from his stare. In the time it takes me to exhale, I feel a pulse, a wave— something inexplicable. It's as if I'm staring into his soul.

A word floats to my consciousness. It's an emotion, and I feel it as strongly as if it was my own: disgust.

His eyes widen, his mouth slackens. I blink, confused by what just happened. Before I can take another breath, he leads his horse from me and hisses, "You are an abomination."

As I watch the two of them leave, I'm consumed with a single thought: *not another ability.*

When our eyes locked, I read his emotion. It was quick, but the impression still lingers.

Emovis. It's what I am now.

Magister Cruz knew what I did, and he'll tell them all. Reading the emotion of another without their consent is an act of indecency. Also, they'll know I possess these two abilities. They'll think I'm even more of a pariah.

By now I should be numb to these discoveries. I shout in frustration, and I don't care who hears me. "So I'm to possess them all? I didn't ask to be a servant of duty!" The prospect makes me want to spend the rest of my days in confinement. It incenses me.

I mount a black-spotted, white colt. I lead him to a swift gallop, hoping the wind will calm me. But all I can do is think about it. How have I not discovered this until now? I've been looking into people's eyes all week.

I fear it'll happen again. It's a dangerous thing, because the next person I see may be Diamond.

When I arrive at Institute, I'm relieved no human is present. Only a pack of wolves lingers at the perimeter of the main plaza. I dismount and turn to thank the colt, but he's already fled because of the wolves.

I cross the shimmering stone to the main entrance. With each step, I convince myself to take another. A delicate concerto greets me when I enter a grand lobby of stone and glass. Several magisters roam the main corridor. I lower my head as

I enter, though I know it won't make me invisible.

If Diamond is here, I'll find her on the uppermost level, where the medica meet after final discussion. Four grand ascensi line the main corridor. A few magisters are waiting for one to arrive. As I pass them, one of them glances over his shoulder. I feel his glare on me. He whispers to the magister next to him. I sense his eyes on me, too, then the others, until all five of them are focused on me.

I walk faster to reach another ascensus, and a wave of anxiety hits me. Its lights are extinguished. It's not in service. I proceed a bit farther and discover the next one is the same. Then I realize only one must be operating since so few will attend today. I have no choice but to return to the first one.

I stare at the ground, terrified of looking at any of them. As their hissing breath echoes, I make a decision: I can either cower, or I can board with them.

The barrier dissolves. None of the magisters move, so I do. I cross the threshold, my eyes burrowing into the ground. As I watch their feet moving to join me, I can feel my heart pounding in my throat.

I can feel their eyes on me.

The barrier seals. There's a collective inhaling of breath as we prepare for the depletion of oxygen. The ascent begins. As our bodies go weightless, my reflexes overpower my will. I look up. My eyes flicker from one magister to the next.

Disgust.

Pity.

Fear.

Their collective emotions invade my senses. I'm reading them all—simultaneously—and they sense it. Their mouths twitch and their hands contract in response.

The ascensus stops. As my feet settle gently on the floor, they all land squarely on their backs with resounding thuds. There's no recognition in their blank, *catatonic* stares.

My pores flood with the sweat of my fear. I still feel their emotions in my bones. I swim in it until my tears blur my vision, and I blink.

A scream rises to my throat. "I need a medicum!"

Two magisters approach from the hall. They trot to my assistance until they recognize me. Then they run faster.

"They have all succumbed to a state of shock. Help them!"

"*You* did this to them!"

"You unleashed your ability of magnos upon them?" the other screams.

"*Please.* You must help them."

I'm afraid to make eyes contact, but one of them positions himself directly in front of me. He stands so close that his long, fuzzy beard brushes my chin, and I can smell tart cherries on his breath. He stares into my eyes, and I know it's happening again. It's quick, but it's enough.

Antipathy.

He takes a few steps in retreat, points a finger at me and

whispers, "Impossible."

"Sir Benjin, what is it?"

"She has invaded my mind."

"Whatever do you mean? She is a magnos."

He stumbles against the wall, shaking his head at the five magisters in the ascensus. Then he turns to me and hisses, "Abomination!"

I turn and run, unable to ignore the word they now both hurl at me. I run until I reach the end of the hall then hop into a conic, metal housing. I wrap my arms and legs around a pole and slide. The female magister watches my descent, her eyes filled with fear.

I reach the bottom, and sprint through the main entrance. I don't stop.

A voice shrieks. My shoulder and cheek smack into something hard. I fall from the impact, and my head lands on the ground with a hard thud. My vision blurs, and I struggle for breath.

I think I hear voices. The ringing in my ears makes them sound muffled. Long, pale hair hovers above me. I see her mouth moving, but I can't understand her words. Her name is Lana.

She moves out of the way, and Diamond appears, waving her hands and arms over my body to heal my wounds. Her soft hands press firmly to my cheeks. My vision clears. The ringing in my ears is gone.

"Rayne." Her voice speaks in a tone meant to soothe. It also hints of concern.

"Diamond, you saw what happened, did you not?" Lana asks, her hair obscuring a face etched with irritation. "Honestly, Rayne, are you mad? You are fortunate I noticed you in time to slow my craft. Though it would have been recompense for what you did to Jhonis had I not."

"Lana, please leave so I can complete my duty. I need to concentrate."

"She is well enough, Diamond. If she is forever cursed with a limp, it will not be payment enough for all she has done."

"You know duty compels me. Now go."

"Diamond."

"Now."

Lana utters an exaggerated sigh then scowls at me. "Next time, Rayne, I will not take care to slow my craft. I suggest you watch your path, for none in this colony will."

"Leave, Lana."

I'm surprised to hear Diamond speaking with such urgency. I feel back to normal, so I'm not sure what she thinks she still needs to do.

Lana sulks away, and sends her craft toward the docking station. Diamond crouches at my feet and extends an arm, holding it out expectantly.

"Do not be daft, Rayne. Take my hand so I can help you to

your feet."

I lift a baffled hand, and she grabs it and hoists me up.

"How many times must I save you?"

I detect a tone of cordiality. I don't dare meet her eyes to confirm it.

"Why do you keep doing it?"

"As I just told Lana, duty compelled me," she says with the slightest hint of a smile on her voice.

I stare at her rounded, dimpled chin as I say, "Duty does not extend to propriety. You were free to leave my side the moment you physically restored me. After everything that happened with Jhonis and last night, why are you here?"

I look away from her before her eyes have a chance to meet mine. I feel her staring at me. It's odd. We have switched roles.

"I am here because I am an apprentice. You know this."

"That is not what I mean."

"Why are *you* here, Rayne?"

"I was actually looking for you…regarding Jhonis. I need to see his condition for myself, and I believed you might help me." I study the curve of her smooth, wide brows so she doesn't notice my avoidance of her eyes.

A few apprentices are arriving, and all of them notice us. Diamond looks around and says, "Come with me."

Before I can respond, she turns and strides to the north end of the plaza. She circles around it, obscuring herself behind the building. I follow her into a colorful garden of native shrubs and wild grasses. She finds a spot behind a large bush, and I sit next to her. As I focus on her pale-yellow foot soles, I'm relieved we're sitting next to each other. It'll be easier to avoid her eyes.

"Are you going to be late for your training?"

"Yes, but they are not expecting me to be here. They have given me a pass to be with Jhonis." Her voice falters at these words, but she continues. "We medica are tending to him in shifts. Since this is not my hour to keep vigil, my parentes urged me to spend my free hours as I normally would. They think it will distract me from my torment."

"How serious is his condition?"

"His ribs are fractured, his lungs are punctured, and his heart is weak. He has not yet stirred from unconsciousness. Though it is dire, there is hope." She brushes her hand on a shrub, seeming to focus on nothing.

"Please believe when I say I am consumed by guilt for what happened to him."

"Why? You did nothing to cause it. If his intentions proved successful, it would be you lying unconscious instead of him." She looks directly at me, and I quickly divert my eyes.

"Everyone who was there saw what Jhonis did, yet they all still blame me."

"And may the universe scourge them for their lies."

I feel her staring at me, waiting for me to say something.

At last she continues. "If I was stronger in resolve, I would have defended you last night. It is just…I could not bring myself to do so while sitting next to Jhonis's parentes. For this I beg your forgiveness."

I feel as though a gush of icy water has splashed my face. I'm drowning in disbelief. Then I remember what she did.

"You *did* defend me. Silently. You did not raise your hand."

"I wondered if you noticed. You must know, Rayne, I have since informed his parentes and the medica of the truth. Soon everyone will know."

"An ally from the most unlikely source," I mutter.

She looks at me, and I divert my eyes to a cactus to feign embarrassment from my statement.

"I have grown weary of his immaturity. All of theirs. I am also done with keeping up pretenses that I share their opinions."

"Since when have you not?"

She shrugs and I can feel her piercing eyes on me. "Since I saw the Great Pine, and the moss, and the wave at the Tank. And let us not forget the Annex. All these miraculous things keep happening, and you are at the center of them all."

My breath seizes, and my impulse is to look at her in shock, yet I train my eyes on my feet. She knows what I've done, yet she's here, talking to me like it's nothing.

"Rayne, I have a question for you."

"What is it?"

"Why do you avoid my eyes when it has always been *you* to dare *me* with your gaze?"

My face flushes. I have no idea how to respond.

"Perhaps it would help if I told you I saw Magister Cruz a short while ago. I heard him and Magister Inira talking about their encounter with you at the brook."

"You know what I did to him," I say, still refusing to look at her.

She nods and says, "Several know by now, I would imagine. What a week this has been for you, yes?"

I'm too baffled to form words. In the midst of everything she knows, she's being amiable. We're huddled together like comrades, so close that I can smell the lily and rose petals she harvests for her perfume.

"Look at me, Rayne."

"There is no need."

She positions herself in front of me. *"Look at me."*

"No," I whisper, my voice hoarse.

She moves closer, forcing me to draw my legs to my chest. "Need I declare it in stark terms? Then I will. I know you possess multiple abilities. Floresca. Aquamarist. Aerisma. Magnos. Do you deny it?"

My eyes dart up at her from shock. She doesn't blink, and before I can try to stop it, her emotions flood my senses.

Compassion.

Empathy.

Regret.

I blink again to break myself from the link. Her emotions surge through me. I expel my breath, trying to clear my mind.

"And now emovis," she says, tilting her head in triumph.

"How do you not fear and loathe me? Do you…also have…"

"Multiple abilities of exponential power? No, I do not."

"Then how can you not despise me as they all do? *They* only know a fraction of what you do." My mouth flutters as I try to make sense of the thoughts swarming in my head.

She lowers her hands from my face and says, "I will answer, but first I am going to help you."

"You mean with Jhonis?"

"No. I mean your inability to control reading emotions."

"How can you?"

"I know how it works. My frater is an emovis, remember? Did your pater or Rafe never discuss it with you?"

I groan and say, "No, they never did."

"I apologize for mentioning them."

"No need."

"If you say so. In any case, this is how it works. As long as you fear what you will discover, you will not be able to control the ability of emovis. You must also master your own emotions. Why do you think the emoves tend to be so stodgy?"

"That is it? That is all I have to do?"

"Simple, yes?"

I regard her with more clarity than I've had in days. I stare into her green eyes, feeling at least a tiny bit of the weight has been lifted.

"Ah, see? Easy."

"Diamond, I still do not understand. With everything you know, how does this not terrify you?"

"I fear nothing, Rayne, save death from the failure of my duty."

"But how are you so calm about it? I find it unfathomable, and it is happening to *me.*"

She stands up and says, "I believe it is a conversation for another day. Right now I need for you to come with me."

"Where?"

"You said you wanted to see Jhonis."

"What about his parentes? They will never allow me to see him."

"Then we simply must ensure they do not know you are there. Come. It is time to set your conscience at ease."

23

I balance my footing on the exposed roots of a Poplar. I press my ear to the cool brick, listening for voices. All I hear are the sounds of nature. I lean my back against the wall and gaze at the mingling of leaves. The green drowns in the autumn colors of orange and red. They've changed a lot this week.

This is the first time I've been on these grounds. I find the normalcy of it to be strange. I imagined it contained only Willows, their drooping form a metaphor to Jhonis's existence.

A soft cough startles me. When I turn to the window, I see Diamond has disengaged it. When I peer into the chamber, only Jhonis is there, lying in his pod.

I don't waste the short time I have. I hoist myself through the frame and land on the floor. His chamber isn't how I thought it would look. I imagined walls as dark as a black hole to match the void of light in his soul. Instead they're a mottle of moss and earthen stone. His pod coverings are silver with hints of pale pink to match the color of his hair. The combination is lovely. Too lovely. I wonder if this room symbolizes the person he wishes himself to be or if his parentes decorated it like this.

As I approach him, I feel awkward. I shouldn't be in his chamber. I don't belong here, but I can't leave. Not yet.

With each strained rise and fall of his chest, my empathy for him increases. It's an emotion I never thought I would apply to him.

I want to help him. I need to help him.

He looks peaceful. I never thought his face was capable of looking as such, not even while unconscious.

As my eyes scan his torso, I ponder the details of his injuries. I almost feel the pain in his body. I don't understand my sudden eagerness to help him. I can't fight it.

I can feel his life force waning with each tug of his breath. It summons me, begging me to act.

My face warms and my hands tingle with unexpected compassion. The longer I stand over him, the more overwhelming the sensation in my hands becomes. I clench them into fists to quiet it, but it only increases.

I can *feel* his lungs and his ribs and his heart. I flex my hands and shake my head to rid myself of it. It doesn't work. It's so strong. It's like I can see the precise location of his internal suffering.

I must mend it. I must heal him.

I lift my tingling hands, now as cold as a brook in the early autumn morn. I place them above his torso. The ache I feel in my chest subsides. A surge of duty releases through me—from me—into him.

My arms dance above him as if enticed by a melody which only they can hear. My hands pulse and wave to their own rhythm.

I sense his breathing steadying. I feel the crackling of his ribs as they mend and the weakness which plagues him dissolving. Strength returns to him.

With each flutter of my arms and hands, the ache in my chest grows fainter until I can no longer feel it at all. The sense of duty is gone. Something else replaces it. Achievement.

The icy tingling in my hands is gone too. As I stare at my palms, something behind them draws my focus. Jhonis's gray eyes are staring at me. He positions himself to a seated position, looking as shocked as I feel.

I hear a gasp to my left as a ceramic vessel shatters on the floor. Diamond is standing there, her mouth slack, her eyes wide and glistening.

"Jhonis, you are awake!" She runs to his side, wrapping

her arms around him and kissing his mouth.

"Diamond," Jhonis says, his voice caked with weariness. "How long have I—"

"Two days. We all feared for you, and now you are restored to us. I cannot wait to tell your parentes."

When she stands to leave, my awkwardness returns. I can't be in here alone with him. I turn to the window and hoist myself up.

"Rayne, wait! Stay."

Diamond's insistence causes me to lower myself to the floor. I sense Jhonis staring at me. I meet his eyes. His obvious confusion mingles with his usual bitterness.

"Diamond, why is she in my chamber?"

"She is here at my request."

"Why would you bring her? Do not tell me you took pity on her guilt." The familiar, seething tone returns to his voice, and I know he truly is healed.

"You know it is not guilt which she feels."

"Of course it is guilt." He shifts forward and glares at me with such loathing that I regret staying.

"Do not strain yourself, Jhonis. Do not focus on negativity."

"Negativity? Was I not nearly dead by her hand? From your expression upon seeing me, I know it is true."

"Jhonis, *please*. There is no need to declare lies."

"*Lies?*"

"I saw you, Jhonis. I saw the whispering words form on your lips. You bid the black stallion to do to her what it acted upon you instead. It is by your words alone that you nearly died. You owe her your gratitude."

"Gratitude?" His shrieking voice makes me press my hands to my ears.

His eyes are fiercer than I've ever seen them. I didn't think it was possible. I press my back against the wall, my hand fumbling for the window threshold.

"Rayne, please. You must stay."

"Let the Sape leave, Diamond. She should never have come."

"Had she not, you would still be unconscious and near death. Is this what you would prefer?"

"What I prefer is for this *Sape* to vacate my chamber—*my grounds*—at once."

"It is *she* who restored you. She has done in a matter of minutes what all of us medica have been trying to accomplish these past two days."

"You think me a fool?" he hisses. "The moment I opened my eyes to see her filthy form next to me, I knew it was she who did so."

"Then why are you behaving like this, Jhonis?"

"You, Diamond, are mad if you think I owe this Sape any level of gratitude. I cringe from her act. I wish to rip from my body all which she restored. I prefer death. It is more tolerable than what I must now endure by her filth. Leave my chamber *now*, Sape, lest I reward you by placing my hands around your neck and consoling my grief through your death."

24

My eyes burn with emotions I can't define. Jhonis's reaction shouldn't surprise me. A growl surfaces in my throat, and I stop running. My scream echoes in the forest, and I regret no one is here to witness it.

I sink to my knees and force my trembling voice to quiet. I focus on my surroundings. The ground is damp. It must have rained sometime before dawn. I sink my hands into the earth. As I grab the soil into my fists, my chest heaving in frustration and exhaustion.

Homo praestans are supposed to behave better than Jhonis just did. We're *supposed* to be masters of self-control. We're not supposed to treat others with malice or threaten the life of another.

It's easy to uphold standards of propriety when everyone is the same. It's another thing to prove it when diversity challenges the norm.

They are hypocrites, but there's nothing I can do to change anyone's opinion of me. These words calm me. I relax in the soil, expelling the negativity through each breath. I focus on the positive. Everyone doesn't hate me. It would be unjust to accuse them all. My mater. Rafe. Sir Theo…Diamond. They don't stand against me.

I stand to my feet and stomp over the terrain. The sound of it soothes me somehow. Jhonis's words no longer sting. I'll forget what he said. I'll forget him.

But can I truly fault him? Any of them? In seven days, I've discovered I possess multiple abilities. *All ten of them.*

"Susurrator. Floresca." I long for the day when I believed I only possessed these two.

"Aerisma. Aquamarist. Terracostos. Ignitor." The abilities of the four elements which I discovered on the Tank.

"Providior." If I were to remain, I would be compelled to provide to all those in my colony who despise me.

"Magnos. Emovis. Medicum." The final three which I discovered in less than a day.

I wonder how I'm able to function, to think, to do anything but lie in a crumble under the weight of what lies within me. Perhaps they're right. I'm an abomination.

Answers. It's an elusive word which exists only in theory. There's no assurance I'll discover anything useful at the Capitolium. It's very likely they'll regard me with as much animosity as my colony.

I don't know what to do. If I continue like this, I'll go mad. Who can I ask for advice?

The answers might lie with Diamond. She knows about more of my abilities than anyone else. The way she reacted convinces me there's something she's not saying. I have no doubt she took me to Jhonis, because she believed I could save him. What does she know about my abilities? I walk aimlessly, frustrated that I can't ask her now, not until she leaves Jhonis's side.

Then there's Sir Theo. He was kind to me when he discovered I was a providior. He's always been kind. If he has no advice to give, I believe—at least—he'll listen.

I survey the section of forest to gauge my location. The Harvesting Center is near, but first I have to let him know I'm coming. I activate my device and say, "Contact the master processor."

The screen changes to green, and Sir Theo appears before me. "Madam Providior. Good day to you." His smile is so warm and genuine that I think he must not have heard anything about Jhonis.

I try to hide my nervousness as I respond. "Good day to you too, Sir Theo."

"How do you fare this day, Madam Providior? I do hope you are well. I have heard rumor of the night you left this place. Of course I do not believe a word they speak. Now tell me, will duty bring you to me this day?"

"No, Sir Theo. I hoped to beg an audience of you regarding, well, Jhonis and…related matters. If you are unable to oblige, I understand entirely."

"Only duty would prevent it, and at present, I have no task to accomplish. Therefore, please do come at once. What is your distance?"

"I am a minute or two by foot."

"Then I will await your knock at the providior entrance."

"I am grateful to you, Sir Theo." I tap my fingers to end the communication and set my feet to a trot.

When I reach the clearing, I see the wooden door is already open. He stands just beyond the threshold. As I approach, his face illuminates with genuine warmth. He ushers me into the room and closes the door behind us. "If you will, Madame Providior, follow me to a more agreeable place where we may converse."

He leads me through the harvesting door, then to another in a dark recess. He opens it, and I follow him into a small, dimly lit room. In the center is a round, wooden table with four matching chairs around it.

"Please, let us sit." He removes a chair from its place and holds out his hand for me.

"Thank you, Sir Theo."

"Let us get to it. No need to pass minutes in pleasantries. I have heard all which occurred, including the events at the amphitheater. Had I been present, I would have declared my opposition and disapproval of them all."

"You were *not* present?" I repeat, realizing it didn't occur to me to search for him.

"I was tending to my nepos so his parentes could attend." As he pauses, his mouth twitches, and his bushy brows flutter. I don't need to invade his thoughts to know it's unease he feels. "I beg of you to tell me something—and do not tend to my sensitivities as a pater."

"Of course, Sir Theo."

"Did you happen to see if my filia raised her hand against you? Forgive me. It is inconsiderate of me to ask. Besides, I suppose you might not have recognized her since you have never met formal acquaintance."

"You could never offend, Sir Theo. However, I cannot speak on it. I did not notice whether she did or not."

As he sighs and nods in acceptance, I choose not to share what I saw. I'm fairly certain all raised their hand except two: my mater and Diamond.

"Very well. I suppose I could beg the question to her directly, but I fear the possibility." He clears his throat and says, "Yes, well, Madam Providior, none shall ever sway my good opinion of you. You are always welcome in my presence, regardless of whomever else occupies it."

"I appreciate your kindness, more than you will ever know."

"Now we have covered this matter, so allow me to rejoice in the most brilliant of discoveries. I declare I was astonished and delighted when I learned you are a magnos such as myself."

The hairs on my arms stand on end, and my jaw slackens in surprise. "So, then you know I possess—"

"Two abilities?—Pardon my interruption. Yes, I do know. It is extraordinary."

"Your convictions place you in the minority, Sir Theo. Most others think…they call me an abomination."

"Pay no heed to anyone who would use such a word against you. They speak only from fear of the undiscovered, because you, Madam Providior, are extraordinary. Do pardon my repeat of this word. I simply cannot summon another to express how remarkable this is."

"I am not sure I agree."

"You must not allow adversity to tarnish this for you. You should celebrate this extra gift which the Luminescence saw fit to bring to you."

"Why would it have done so? Or, perhaps it did not. Perhaps there is something else to this."

"How do you mean?"

"None of this makes any sense." My thoughts drift to the

night of the trampling and my near-death experience. "I have to tell you something, and I hope you can keep it in confidence."

"Certainly. I vow it."

I nod and continue. "The night of the horrific incident with Jhonis, I found myself at one of the lightning fields."

"*Madam Providior.* Surely you were not so distraught that you would seek such danger."

"No. Not exactly. You see, I was convinced our colony would banish the black stallion. Therefore, I thought I owed it to him to be the one to whisper. He led us near there. I sent him away before we got too close."

"I do hope you departed most hastily."

"I wish I had, but I did not. My anguish fed my curiosity. I preferred it. I needed to erase the images. I ended up wandering in the field until…I slipped…into an energy pool."

"Great cosmos!" His mouth hangs open, his eyes wide with terror and awe.

"I was submerged for a while, and I could not move. I do not know how long I was there before I was rescued."

"Rescued! How? By *whom?*"

"If I were to tell you now, I believe it would prove too much for you to bear. In any case, my question is this. The following night, I went to the amphitheater. It is when I discovered the ability of magnos. The sensation was the same as when I was in the pool. So…" I pause. I'm not quite sure how to ask the question so he'll understand. He waits for me to compose my thoughts, the lines in his face creased with worry.

I lower my eyes to the table, feeling guilty for causing him such concern when our relations are so new. I force myself to continue. "I suppose I want to know if, when you perform your ability, do you feel an electromagnetic surge pulsing through you?"

"Only slightly, Madam Providior, and this further astounds me. And what I know to be certain with no degree of uncertainty is this. It is impossible for any living creature to survive submersion in one of those energy pools. Not for one second. Not at all. How you lived to recount it, I cannot fathom. It is miraculous." The corners of his eyes and mouth twitch. He studies me as if he doesn't believe I'm alive.

"I wonder if—because of the Luminescence—the pools aren't lethal to humans."

"Oh, but they are. I assure you. The data is irrefutable."

"There must be some explanation for how I survived. Maybe the answer lies in my heightened abilities."

"You pose an intriguing concept, Madam Providior. Intriguing indeed." He reclines in his chair, cupping his hand to his chin to consider my words. He sighs, shakes his head, and says, "I suppose the proof of your theory is as evident as your presence in this room. If another explanation exists, I am ignorant of it."

"Perhaps we already know it."

"How so?"

"Regardless of the word they choose to use, what if their sentiments are correct? What if I am an unnatural being? I survived due to whatever preternatural defect courses through my veins."

"I shall not allow you to declare such a thing against yourself, Madam Providior." He plants his hands on the table and leans toward me, then flinches from the act and withdraws. "Pardon me, but you must know none of this would be possible if nature did not bestow it upon you."

"How can you speak with such certainty, Sir Theo?"

"I am staring at the proof. Consider the evolution of human beings. Perhaps you are merely the first of a new kind. Yes…it could be so," he nods, mostly to himself.

"You mean to imply I am a new species of human?"

"I only speak in conjecture, but perhaps a mutation of your DNA has made you more grand than us all."

"More grand." I don't know whether to laugh, sigh, or scoff. The sound I make is a combination of all three. "I appreciate you more than you will ever know, Sir Theo."

"Have you spoken to your parentes of this? Surely they can provide counsel as well."

"Unfortunately, they cannot."

"Very well, then perhaps you might seek answers from a source more qualified than either myself or your parentes."

"Whom do you suggest?"

"Hmm," he begins, tilting his head and scratching his bearded face. "Your situation is unprecedented. Personally, I know of no person in this colony who might possess adequate knowledge on this issue."

"Then there are no answers for me to discover. Is this your assessment?"

"No, no. You misinterpret. While I do not believe such a person exists in this colony, or province for that matter, the answers you seek might very well lie in the East."

"In the Capitolium."

"I believe so."

"I considered the same, but what if we are both wrong?"

"Unless you wish to spend your days on this Earth regretting the unsolved, I believe you must go. If you do and none there can offer the resolution you seek, at least you would have tried."

I release a deep sigh in consent. He's right. "Then to the Capitolium I will go."

He reclines in his chair and offers a smile teetering on joy and dismay. "Very well, Madam Providior. I am not abashed to state my regret at your necessary departure. I shall only have the pleasure of your services for a matter of—when do you come of age? Pardon my insubordination, Madam Providior. I do not mean to offend."

"You could never offend, Sir Theo. I will be of age in less than three weeks."

"Then I will hope you are called to duty often until then."

"I hope so as well."

"If not, I invite you to call upon me if you wish to discuss this or anything else. I cannot begin to fathom what you must endure each hour of the day."

I have avoided telling him my full truth until now. He regards me with such sincerity, that I decide it's time.

"You only know the slightest bit of it, I am afraid."

"How do you mean?"

As I consider how to begin, I'm drawn to the warmth in his eyes. What I do next isn't from fear of what he might think of me. It's from worry that I'll discover none in the Capitolium as kind and supportive as he is. I linger, and I forget myself. I invade him.

Admiration.

Respect.

Adoration.

Compassion.

I force myself to stop.

His eyes widen and his brows raise in incredulity. "By all the stars in the universe. *Another* ability." He claps his hands in glee, erasing the guilt I feel. "You have withheld some extraordinary details from me, Madam Providior. Remarkable."

"Forgive me, Sir Theo. I should not have invaded you."

"To the seas with such notions. Three abilities!"

"Ten, actually. I possess all ten. Before I came here, I discovered the final one. Medicum."

"Great cosmos!" He scrambles from his chair, nearly knocking it to the floor. "Allow me to guess. Jhonis?"

"Yes. He is awake."

He claps his hands again and releases a booming laugh. "All ten abilities. This is spectacular."

"Sir Theo, how can you still think so? This does not dampen your opinion of me in the slightest?"

"On the contrary, Madam Providior. I think you more extraordinary. How any of this is possible is presently inconsequential to me. I should be content to await the day you learn the truth of it all. If—of course—you would deign to share it with me."

"Of course, I will. You will never know how grateful I am to you. The admiration you feel toward me is mutual."

"You flatter me greatly, Madam Providior."

I push out my chair and stand to my feet. Without thinking, I do something outside the boundaries of propriety. I wrap my arms around him and squeeze, then kiss him on the cheek. He smells of fresh vanilla bean.

His hands lightly pat my back, and I regain my composure. "Forgive me, Sir Theo. I do not mean to unsettle you. I only mean to thank you."

"No, no, you have not. It is just…you are…extraordinary. There is that word again."

He laughs at himself now, and I feel hopeful. Knowing

there's a person who exists who regards me like this is
enough to suppress my worry. He's given me the reassurance
to seek answers, and the confidence to accept it if there are
none.

25

As I stroll through the plaza, I'm refreshed. Somehow I manage to suppress the bitter declarations which male and female voices hurl at me. Their words have no impact. Their opinions mean nothing. My existence warrants neither fear nor disgust from anyone. I'm not an abomination. For this, I'm indebted to Sir Theo.

I enter the forest to return to my villa. It's past midday, so my mater will be there by now. My stomach anticipates whatever sustenance she will have for me. My pater likely hopes I won't return. I find myself apathetic about disappointing him. I now consider him the same as the others in this colony who despise me. Given the hour, I think of the Tower and Rafe. It's absurd to think he'll be there.

When I see my villa ahead, my hunger increases. I trot up the veranda steps. The glass barrier is already deactivated. It's a pleasant day, so my mater must have left it open to the warm breeze.

As I enter the culina, I hear my pater's voice. I can't tell what he's saying. I almost want to leave, but instead I open the cold storage, hoping to find a prepared dish. Before I can select something, I freeze from the sound of another male voice. I don't recognize it.

I close the door to the cold storage, and when I enter the corridor, I hear my mater's voice too. They're all in the salon. I conceal myself among the Aspens as I creep closer. When I can discern their words, I stop and stifle the sound of my breath.

"Yes, but I still do not understand the cause for failing to inform us." My pater speaks in such a tone of respectful defiance that I wonder who the guest is.

"Roman, please."

"Worry not, Lady Sapphire. I understand the frustration you both must feel. However, I assure you it was necessary."

The unfamiliar voice is too amplified to be in the salon. My parentes must be engaged in a communication through one of their devices. My heart pounds with such intensity, I can feel it in my chest. I'm anxious to learn his identity, but I convinced they'll stop talking if I show myself.

"Respectu, Councilor, keeping us ignorant only served to cause strife in our domus. Had you informed us, these past fifteen years might have been…I would not have behaved…" My pater doesn't complete his sentence. His voice cracks, and I can hear his sobs.

"May I ask why we were not informed, Councilor?" My mater asks. "Do pardon my insistence in knowing the details, but we feel it is warranted at this juncture."

"I regret to inform you I am unauthorized to provide you with more information than I already have. The important thing for you both to understand is our gratitude for your task well accomplished. You nurtured her to be a person of solid character, and now your duty to us—to her—is complete."

"Surely you cannot expect me to cease communication with her. I will forever regard her as my filia."

"You refer only to yourself, Sapphire?"

"My words are not intended to shame you, Roman."

"Please, Sir Roman. Lady Sapphire. None of us expects either of you to abandon your parental regard for her. However, please understand communication with her after she comes of age will not be possible."

"*Why,* Councilor? Why must we remain ignorant of all this? What do you intend for her?"

"Again, Sir Roman, I regret to inform you I cannot elaborate. What information I have provided is a courtesy."

Silence. Someone clears a throat. Someone sighs.

"Will we ever see her again, Councilor? Can you at least tell us this?"

"Forgive me, Lady Sapphire, but I cannot answer, since I do not know."

"This is madness. How can you not know? Do pardon my insolence, but it truly is madness."

"I must agree with my husband, though his manner of expressing it is in want of decorum."

"His choice of words is merely the expression of his emotions, and I do not fault him for such. Now, I would like to move forward as I must attend to other duties this day. Therefore, allow me to address *you,* Sir Rafe."

I nearly choke on a gasp. I press my hand to my mouth to silence my breath.

"Yes, Councilor."

"We are also pleased with your service these past five years. You have continued to impress us since the first day of your recruitment. We did well to select you for the role of her comrade."

I feel as though I've been punched in the chest. I fight the pounding in my ears as I force myself to listen.

"Thank you, Councilor. However, I must remind you my comradeship with Rayne has been diminished of late. I know it is not as you wish."

"The events of this past week are inconsequential. In essence, the rift between the two of you proves advantageous. It serves to make her parting easier. Now, unless any of you has anything further to report, I will conclude this communication. Sir Roman and Lady Sapphire, one of us will contact you in ten days to schedule her departure, wherein we will escort her to the Capitolium.”

“Would it not be possible for me to escort her, Councilor?”

“I regret I must deny your request, Lady Sapphire. We feel it would serve her best to bid farewell while in the familiarity of her colony. It will be easier for her to adjust once she arrives if she has already parted with all ties to her life as a subordinate citizen. I understand your emotional bond, so I will remind you of this. There are just under three weeks remaining. I suggest you pass it in familial significance. Now, I must bid you farewell. Good day to you all.”

“Good day, Councilor.”

As the three voices speak in unison, my legs weaken. The Aspen leaves rustle from my weight as I stumble to my knees. I can’t breathe. I clutch my chest, indifferent to the fact that my wheezing echoes in the corridor.

“Rayne!”

Through eyes flooded with tears, I watch the form of Rafe approach me. His face is suffused with shock.

I grab the nearest trunk and pull myself to my feet. A tremor consumes me. It feels as though crawling insects plague my flesh.

My parentes appear in the corridor. Their eyes are saturated with guilt. I focus on my mater. I want her to know I'm not angry with her. It's Rafe who I newly despise. He extends a hand to my shoulder. I retreat and release my anger in a single sentence. "Never be so bold as to touch me again."

"Rayne, *please.* Allow me to explain."

"I loathe the sound of your voice. I will not heed the words of a liar!" I scream as I back away from him.

"Please!"

I push past him and my parentes, bumping into the trees in my haste to escape. I wave my hand over the entrance panel. It feels like an eternity before it deactivates the barrier. I hear him calling to me. I hear my parentes calling my name. I ignore them all as I run down the path and into the cover of trees.

My mind is bombarded by all I heard, yet the only thing I can focus on is the betrayal.

It was all a lie. Our comradeship was false. His affections were contrived. Each time he put his arm around me and pulled me close for an embrace was a lie.

He yells to me. I hear his rapid footfall trampling the ground to catch me. He won't. My lead is too great.

I run faster to smother the ache in my heart. It only increases with each step.

I stop running. My anguish compels me. I must face him.

This time will be the last.

As I wait for him to reach me, I lift my face to the sky. I close my eyes and do something I haven't done for days.

I whisper.

I feel Rafe standing beside me. I want to strike his deceitful face with the force of my glare. I hate him—the sight of him and the smell of him.

"Rayne, allow me to speak, I beg of you."

"You wish me to entertain your lies?"

"Not lies, Rayne. Upon my honor, I will only speak truth."

My hands contract into fists, and I imagine myself using them against him. My words will strike with greater force than my fists ever could. I tell myself this though I don't believe either would do justice. My words are unlikely to injure a person who was recruited to be my comrade. Still I spit the words which force themselves from my lips.

"The sight of you repulses me. All I feel for you is pure, insatiable loathing. I will spew all contents of my stomach if I am forced to remain in your presence any longer."

"If I could remove all your suffering, I would. I hope to begin to mend it with what I will say now." He steps closer to me. I feel his energy, hear his breath as he lifts his hands and places them on my shoulders.

My flesh writhes from his touch. I lift my arms to fling his hands from me. "I only said you may speak. Do *not* touch me."

I sense him trying to force my eyes to meet his gaze, but I won't relent.

"Rayne, please."

"Every memory I have of you is false. Every word you ever spoke to me, every time you came to my defense, every time you offered me the warmth of your embrace is plagued with what someone ordered you to do."

"You are *wrong,* Rayne. Yes, it is true I was recruited. However, it ceased to be duty the first day we met. My affections toward you were always genuine."

"Still you lie. I heard the words you spoke to the councilor."

"I do not lie. It was my privilege to be your comrade. *Is.* This I swear upon all the stars in the infinite universe. Look at me and tell me you do not believe me."

"Look at you? Why? So you might invade my emotions?"

"Why would you—Have I ever done so?"

I don't respond. Instead I turn from him, lift my face to the sky, and whisper.

"Have I ever done so?"

I groan at his insistence and mutter, "It does not matter."

"It *does* matter, Rayne. Please, tell me there is hope. Please tell me I have not lost the privilege of your comradeship."

There is a way for me to gage the truth. I could simply read *his* emotions. Why should I care about invading him after what I now know? I could learn with certainty what he thinks of me. I could discover the cause for every embrace, every warm gaze, but I won't. None of it would have occurred had he not been recruited. All of those moments were fabricated. The sum of our history together is a farce.

He lifts his hands. His fingertips graze my shoulders, and I shudder at his touch. I have to end this now. There's nothing he can say.

"Make no further attempts to touch me, Rafe. Make no further attempts to speak to me. Your words mean nothing. *You* mean nothing."

"Please."

"Any attempt will be futile. In less than three weeks, I will be gone for good. I long for the day to arrive."

Without further word, I turn from him and run.

"Rayne!"

I hear him behind me, but I already have the lead. He won't catch me.

I run through the trees, leaping over a stream in my path, dodging rocks and shrubbery.

I whisper.

I come to a Great Ash with a low-hanging branch. I grab onto it and climb.

"Rayne!"

His hand brushes my ankles, and I climb faster. I stretch to meet the next branch, and I pull myself onto it.

Again I whisper.

The branches sway under my footing, and I grab onto the trunk to balance myself. When I break through the canopy, my real comrade is there waiting for me. When he sees me, he presents his back. As I mount, I feel a hand brushing my ankle.

"Take me from this place, Master Eagle."

He jerks his beak in accord and spreads his wings. I wrap my arms around him as he climbs. Then I hear a voice calling to me from the trees.

"Rayne! I love you!"

26

I don't know whether it's the vertical angle of our flight or the weight of those words which send my heart plummeting to the ground. I tighten my grip around the master eagle. I consider whispering to him to return to the trees and to Rafe. I almost do, but I can't. The councilor's words save me from the mistake.

The master eagle levels his flight. I lean forward to adjust, burying my face in his back. The briskness of autumn causes me to seek warmth in his feathers. My eyes begin to water. It doesn't matter whether it's from the wind or what just happened. With each beat of the great wings, I begin to feel free.

The Board can't come for me fast enough. I have no desire

to spend these weeks knowing Rafe might try to see me. I wish I could leave now.

As the wind beats my face, I wonder why I have to wait. I don't need them to come for me. I have a way to get to them. All I'd have to do is bid the master eagle to carry me east.

As soon as I think it, I realize it's an impulse I can't indulge, at least not right now. I can't go without first seeing my mater. I owe her this.

My pater deserves nothing from me. Though he wept in the presence of the councilor, his regret was tainted. Affected. His sentiment was clear. It almost offends me. He could have loved me had he known everything. Conditional love is not love.

Though my pater will be with her, I have to return to my domus. My mater deserves a proper farewell. Seeing her is worth the risk of bearing the sight of my pater.

"Master Eagle, I bid you to escort me to my villa, but please meander in your course. I wish to remain up here with you a while longer."

He utters an assenting cry. As he leans to the left to begin our return, I'm still conflicted. I told Sir Theo I would visit him before I left. Never did I think it would be today. Though he would argue it's not so, I can't usurp his time twice in one day. I decide to do something else.

I tap my fingers to activate my device. I don't know if it'll even function at this height. The notion is silenced when a glowing screen appears before me, hovering against the blue sky.

"Call the master processor."

The screen turns green, and after a few moments, Sir Theo appears before me.

"Madam Providior. Good afternoon. Has duty called you so quickly?" He squints as he speaks, tilting his head to see around me.

"No, Sir Theo."

"Well, then you honor me by your communication. To what might I attribute it? Have you more questions for me? News to share—Pardon me…Madam Providior, something odd is occurring with my field. It almost looks as though you are floating. Where are you now, if I might ask?"

"Nothing is the matter with your field, Sir Theo. Tell me something, do you currently have it set at its optimal width?" I already know the answer. If he did, he would see exactly where I am.

"No, I do not. Pardon me while I—Great cosmos!"

He leaps backward, fumbling to steady himself against a wall. He takes a few timid steps forward, narrowing his eyes. I stifle a smile, imagining what it must look like on his end of the communication.

"By all the stars in the universe…How did you…"

"The master eagle answered the call of my whisper."

"I should not be surprised. Extraordinary, Madam

Providior. It is a word which suits you more than ever."

"Sir Theo, I wanted to inform you of something."

"What is it, Madam Providior?" As he speaks, he doesn't look at me but around me.

"I am leaving the colony…this day. You are the first to know."

Now he looks at me directly, his face slack with surprise. "Whatever for, Madam Providior?"

"Firstly, I will inform you a councilor held conference with my parentes just now. It is the intention of the Board to escort me to the Capitolium when I come of age."

"Then what is the cause for your premature departure? Why would you not await them?"

"Sir Theo…I have no desire to soil the hopes of my future by spending it amongst those who wish me ill."

"But Madam Providior, you are not yet of age. Please forgive me for saying so, but…I do not understand."

"I believe I am close enough."

"Yes…Well, I suppose. You say I am the first to know. Are you certain your parentes will grant your desire?"

"I do not need them to do so."

He says nothing. I can tell he's studying me. He must know I'm resolute, because a smile creeps to his mouth. "Yes. I suppose you do not need their permission. How do you plan to travel such a dist—Ah, of course. Your means shall be none other than the magnificent creature who carries you now."

"Yes, Sir Theo." The master eagle alters our course again. The time for meandering is at an end. "I am en route to my villa, so I must wish you farewell."

"Yes…Very well. I do hope our paths shall once again cross."

"Of course they will. It is simply a matter of when."

He gazes at his field, once again not looking at me but beyond me. "It is splendid."

"What is, Sir Theo?"

"Never before have I witnessed such an exquisite view of the open sky."

"I wish you could see it from where I sit."

He chuckles and says, "I am content with this view. Well…I suppose there is nothing left to us but to say farewell, Madam Providior. I wish you favorable travels and an unimpeded road to discoveries in the Capitolium."

"Thank you for all you have done for me. I will never forget your kindness. Farewell, Sir Theo."

When I end the communication, a sad smile creeps to my face. I truly will miss him.

An odd thought occurs to me. I should go to Diamond to thank her for her kindness. I dismiss it as quickly as it arrives. I expect she'll be with Jhonis, regardless of his behavior. There's only one place left for me to go.

"Master Eagle, it is time for me to return to land."

With a smooth stroke of his wings, our flight descends.

The tapestry of muted green, orange, and red becomes more defined. He swoops toward the Willows on my grounds. By now he knows precisely where to take me.

He levels his path and descends into the clearing. I dismount and turn to him to stroke his chest. "I will be honored if you await my return, Master Eagle. However, I am not certain how long I will be. Will you oblige?"

He jerks his beak and lowers his head. I caress his wing in gratitude then leave him waiting for me.

When I enter through the culina, all is silent. Suddenly I'm worried. If she's not here, I'll have to wait for her to return.

I creep along in case she's resting in the salon. A stream of light spills into the corridor. The source is the window in my chamber.

As I approach, I hear faint sniffles. I peek inside and find my mater standing next to my pod. I watch as she slides her hand over the fabric. She leans forward to adjust my cushion, then picks it up and holds it to her chest. She wraps her arms around it and caresses it with her cheek.

I whisper with a voice I didn't expect to sound so hoarse. "Mater."

"Rayne!"

I feel guilty for invading her like this. Never before have I witnessed her so vulnerable. She drops the cushion on my pod as I enter.

"Forgive me for encroaching on your privacy, dear Rayne.

I only meant to—"

"You have nothing to explain, Mater. I am pleased to find you here, actually."

"Are you all right?" Her trim brows furrow on her forehead with concern.

"Yes, Mater."

"I did not think I would see you again this day. If you are angry with me, you would be more than justified."

"I am not angry with you, Mater. I vow it."

"What of your pater? I suppose I should first ask, of how much of the communication are you privy?"

"I heard all from the moment he wept."

"You must be more specific. Which instance?"

Now *my* brows are raised. I try to imagine this, but I can't. He wept more than once in the presence of a councilor.

"Rayne, you must know your pater truly is penitent."

"Of course he is. He wept from mourning the many instances he could have boasted to all who would listen. He wept because he missed the chance to revel in admiration of being the pater of someone who would fulfill her duty in the Capitolium. He wept for an ego which could have been so much more inflated had he known everything from the day of my adoption."

I stare at the ground in disappointment. I don't want to spend these final moments with my mater drowning in bitterness toward my pater.

"You are justified to feel that way, and I will not dispute it. However, please forgive me for stating I believe you have it wrong—at least in part."

She offers a forced smile, and I shake my head. I know what I heard.

"He is not near, is he?"

"No. He departed not long after you."

"Will he return soon?"

"I suspect not. Your pater wants everyone to know they should alter their opinion of you just as he has. He was eager to attest to his newfound reason for paternal pride."

"I am glad he is not here," I say with a shrug. "So what else did the councilor say?"

A long sigh escapes her as she tilts her head. Her reaction makes me nervous. "We were instructed to say nothing. The Board wishes to enlighten you of everything themselves, whatever it may be. However…"

"Yes?"

"What I have been instructed to do and what I will do are not the same. Why should I be obligated to honor their request when they do not honor mine?" She says this more to herself than to me.

"You refer to escorting me to the Capitolium?"

She nods and sighs again then looks at me with such determination that I flinch in surprise. "I will confess all. The beginning is always the most prudent place to start, so forgive me for stating that which you already know. When your pater and I were in our fourth year of matrimony, I discovered I could bear no children.”

“Yes,” I nod. “This is why you applied to adopt.”

“Yes, we applied. However, the process for us was different than the norm. We did not have the opportunity to choose which child we would welcome to our domus. When we were notified of our approval, we were informed that based on our character and ability profiles, we were selected to care for a particular child who would be most likely to thrive with us. We were told it was a great honor.”

“I suppose *he* loved hearing this—until two years passed and reality proved otherwise.” My mater hunches her shoulders and lowers her head. “Forgive me, Mater.”

“There is no need to apologize.”

“Please, continue.”

“Well, here is the truth of it. Your pater and I were never apprised either to the details of your birth or your parentes natural. Nor were we informed the Luminescence would never come to you—more precisely, that it would come your seventeenth year.”

“Why were you never informed? It is evident now the Board always knew this would happen.”

“I assume, but I have no confirmation this is true.”

“You mean there is a chance the Board did not know? The councilor failed to say?”

"It is apparent they knew something. How much is in question. It is difficult to assess. His reaction to all we stated was impassive."

"He told you I would soon learn all. It must mean they know everything."

"I suppose."

"Did the councilor say when I would find out?"

"He told us their protocol was first to acclimate you to the Capitolium, then make disclosures. He said it would help ease the transition."

"What harm would it do if I learned the reason for all this before I left?"

She shakes her head and says, "You now know as much as your pater, Rafe, and I. It was not a long communication. The councilor passed most of the time listening and then thanking us all for our service. It was clear he never intended to divulge much. We still do not know why any of this happened to you. If the Board knew it would occur this way, the councilor did not inform us."

"Then there is only one way to learn the truth. I must go the Capitolium. And Mater, I vow to confide all."

"Until then, we must be content with what is to come. And Rayne, share this information with no one."

"With whom do you think I might?"

"Just please divulge nothing. Although many in this colony know you possess two abilities, they are not aware there are more. It is best you say nothing. The councilor stated this when we informed him of the events of this week.”

“Oh, Mater, there is much you do not yet know.”

Before she can question me, I take her hand and invite her to sit with me on my pod. I listen to the words pouring from my mouth as I recount everything from the moment I awoke on my day of birth. The only thing I withhold is the lightning farm.

When I finish, I find it difficult to look at her. We sit in silence for so long that I wonder if my pater will return and disrupt us.

Finally, she speaks. “All ten abilities…If the Board knew this would occur—*surely* they must have,” she shakes her head, her lips struggling to form her words. “I hope they did not know.”

“Why?”

“Because if they did, never did I fathom them capable of harboring such a secret from society.”

“I hope they are capable. Otherwise, who will have the answers I seek?”

My mater lifts her head and regards me with such warmth that I melt. “Dear Rayne, I can always depend upon you to view the world through eyes filled with hope.”

She wraps her arms around me, and I wish we could remain like this forever. But I need to leave. I can’t wait for answers. And even if they Board says I can’t come back here, there’s no way I’ll let them stop me, not when I can fly on the back of a master eagle.

"Mater…"

"Yes, dear Rayne?"

"I have to learn the answers to all this. Now."

She pulls from me and stares into my eyes with utter sternness. I finally understand how my pater must feel each time she regards him this way. "Please tell me I misunderstand your meaning."

"You do not. This is the moment in which we must say farewell. Not indefinitely as the councilor alluded. I will return as soon as—"

"You are mistaken. You are not at liberty to quit our domus until you are of age."

"After everything that has happened to me this week, I think I have earned the right to decide."

"Please, Rayne. Do not allow anyone in the colony to force you prematurely from those of us who care for you. What about your pater? Surely you will not leave without first speaking to him."

"There is nothing I wish either to say to him or hear him say to me."

She presses her lips so tightly they become pale. She relaxes them to speak words I despise. "What about Rafe? Do you truly have no desire to mend your comradeship? He has finally confessed his feelings of adoration, and surely you understand his position with the Board. Also, I believe he would have confessed his love sooner, if not for your status of sub-ordinate citizen. It would have been improper for him to do so."

"You mean to tell me you *knew?*"

"I suspected. I was courted in my youth, I will remind you."

"It makes no difference, Mater. Whether I remain for three weeks or leave now has no bearing on what words I will share with him. We have spoken our last. He was *recruited,* Mater. Any trust I had in our comradeship…all of our history together is forever ruined."

"What of forgiveness, Rayne?"

"It is no matter of forgiveness, Mater—Please. I do not wish to waste these moments discussing him."

"Moments. Tell me, Rayne, how do you intend to travel to the Capitolium?"

"You forget my comrade of the skies."

"Where will you go? Accommodations have yet to be es-tablished for you."

"Then I will depend upon you to alert them of my early arrival so they may be ready for me."

"Dear Rayne, is there nothing I can say to sway you to remain until you are of age?"

"Remaining only serves to force us to suffer farewells again. I know I could not bear it, Mater. Please understand why I must go now."

"Why not leave on the morrow? It will afford you travels in the light of day. It will be sunset soon, Rayne. I cannot bear the thought of you traveling the skies in the darkness of night."

"After all I have confessed, you are concerned about me being on the back of the master eagle at night? Besides, he sleeps and rises with the sun."

"Then why would you leave now, knowing you will have no place to sleep?"

"Whatever do you mean, Mater? I will sleep where he sleeps. It will be the initiation of my adventure."

To this she has no response. She allows a hint of a smile to brighten her face still taut with worry.

"Dear Rayne."

"Mater?"

"I…love you. I always have, though I have never known how to manifest it properly."

"I love you too."

"Please believe me when I say this. Actually, I bid you to read my emotions so you may know what I will say is the utter truth."

"There is no need. I trust you, Mater."

"Very well. I am proud of you, and I have always been. You have shown utter grace all these years where others could never have done so. *I* never could have done so."

My mouth bursts open from the force of my tears, and I

struggle to respond. "You will never know how much your words mean to me. I will carry them with me on my journey east. Trust me when I say I will see you again. I vow it."

This time her smile is uninhibited. She brushes her hand through my hair, looks at me with determination and says, "I will be at peace with your departure this day, only if you agree to something. It has nothing to do either with your pater or Rafe. You must allow me to prepare a proper farewell feast for you and send you with the remaining portions. You must also allow me to prepare a satchel of belongings. Otherwise, I regret I will have no choice but to fly on the back of the master eagle with you."

"Mirificus. I hoped you would offer."

27

It's been an hour since the last light of day faded to darkness. I nestle in a mountain cave, several kilometers west of
the amphitheater. The gentle slopes of the foothills surround
me. I adjust my satchel beneath my head and curl into a ball.
Now that I'm up here lying on a rock floor and dirt, I long for
the comfort of my pod. It's too late. Returning will only give
my mater false hope that I'll stay the three weeks. Besides, my
transportation is asleep.

It seems like our first encounter was a lifetime ago. It's
merely been a week since I awoke to this new existence. Susurrator. Floresca. Aquamarist. Aerisma. Terracostos. Ignitor.
Providior. Magnos. Emovis. Medicum.

This is the order in which I discovered them all. I should feel as though I will burst, but I don't anymore. Up here, I'm free from the calls of duty.

As I imagine what I'll discover in the Capitolium, my eyelids grow heavy.

Darkness blankets me.

~~~

I wake up, unsure how long I've been asleep. The air feels crisp on my face. The ground is cold and unyielding. When I shift to my side in search of comfort, I realize an expansive wing covers me. I bury my head and breathe the scent of his warmth. My eyes close again, a weary smile creases the corners of my mouth, and then I dream.

It seems like mere minutes have passed when the delicate light of morn stirs me. Relishing the final traces of sleep, I don't move. When I sense the gentle rise and fall of my head and shoulders, I realize the surface has changed. Somehow during the night, I came to be cuddled against the master eagle, under the cover of his wing.

When I shift to look at him, I see he's already awake. It's his hour of rising—his hour of hunting.

"Salvē, Master Eagle. You have offered me your warmth in the night. You are a true comrade."

He ruffles his feathers, blocking the early light from spill-
~~~

ing into the cave.

"It seems my sleep has delayed you from fetching your morning fare. Forgive me."

He only peers at me.

"I will be content to await your return, however long it may be. When you do so, are you still willing to carry me to the East? It is a great distance."

This time he jerks his beak in a nod.

"Thank you, Master Eagle. I owe you more than I could ever repay."

He shifts toward the edge of the cave to prepare for flight. "Fly free and majestic this morn."

He nods again, dives from the cave, and flaps his massive wings. I watch him until my stomach reminds me I should eat myself.

I retrieve a vessel of water and sack of eggs, fruit, and cured boar hind. I devour it all in minutes.

I sift through the satchel and smile at the various items which my mater packed for me: enough nourishment for the course of a week, though my journey will last a single day; two pairs of full-length foot soles in case the pair I wear meet some destructive fate; five sets of cold-weather garments; the vessel of water; my face paint; the blue top which I wore on my day of birth; my mouth brush and gel.

I warned her it was too much, but she reminded me the master eagle could bear the large bundle. For the second time since perusing the contents, I smile at her omission of any tools to bind my hair. Never did she suggest I cut it for my journey. Finally, she truly understands me.

I don't know how long the master eagle will be. I secure my satchel so I'll be ready to leave when he returns. I place it next to me and sit at the edge of the cave, my legs dangling over the steep slope.

My swinging legs cause a few rocks to tumble along the face of the mountain. The first evergreen trees grow several meters below where I sit. Along the way are only rocks and soil and shrubbery.

I'm relieved I can't see the horizon or forest of my colony. But I still can't help wondering what they're doing. I force thoughts of Rafe from my mind and the last words he spoke to me. I have to forget him.

A shadow forms on the crest of a peak in the shape of wings. My comrade returns. As he dives for me, I position the satchel across my shoulder and extend my arms in anticipation.

He descends to the cave and hovers while I hop onto his back. I wrap my arms around him, and he points his beak upward and climbs.

The wind whips my face. I have grown fond of the sensation. I don't need to direct him. He already knows where we're going. Yet, as I witness the view of the foothills, I have a sudden urge to see it all. Until now, I have never travelled farther west than the amphitheater. I don't know when I'll have this chance again.

I lean forward and whisper, "Master Eagle, before we set our course east, might you carry me westward? I wish to view the Great Mountains as you see them. I desire to witness the fullness of their splendor."

He gives a high-pitched sound of assent. My flesh tingles from excitement as he begins his path over the majestic peaks. I venture to look down and laugh at myself for squealing in delight. This is his domain, and he shares it with me.

He flies with such speed that we cross the range in what feels like minutes. It must have been longer, because the sun is higher in the sky. It's all so amazing, it seems to pass too quickly. I feel like a child testing a zephyr-board for the first time. I never want this to end.

The master eagle changes his course upward, and I cling to him, excited for wherever he'll go next. He continues, taking us much higher than ever. My grip grows tighter as the weight of gravity pulls me downward. My heart pounds in my chest from wild anticipation.

We travel upward still. My lungs feel weak and my head feels light from the depletion of oxygen. My grip falters, and I bite my tongue in my first moment of panic. It's fleeting. If I fall, I know he'll dive to catch me.

Struggling to keep my body forward, my arms grow weak. It would be easy if I wasn't carrying this cumbersome satchel.

He must sense my efforts. He points his beak to the horizon, and I feel weightless for a second before I sink, wrapping my arms tighter around his neck.

It's difficult to breathe. I wonder why he's taken us so high. When he levels his flight, I open my mouth to insist he dive lower. A sharp pain in my leg—a scraping sensation—causes me to wince instead.

I jerk my leg upward and torque my body to see it. I place my hand on the source of pain. I flinch from the heat of my touch. I look down in search of what caused it and notice something. My fingers are smeared with my blood.

Before I can beckon the master eagle to return us to the ground, he dives beneath the clouds and slows his pace. He flaps his wings and descends as if he's about to land. The only thing below us is more clouds.

Then he perches—or not. We're hovering in the clouds, yet his feet seem to be planted on the air as if it's solid. He lowers his wings to his sides, and he stands as still as if we're on the ground.

"What…"

He twists his head toward me, then points his beak downward. He repeats the motion until I look down too. What I see makes me think I'm dreaming. His large feet are flat in the sky like it's a solid surface.

He lowers himself and plants his body in a cloud. I lean to the side and extend my hand downward until my fingertips reach the point where he rests comfortably—on nothing. There's only air and mist. Then I feel something as rough as stone.

I chose to trust my hands and ignore my eyes. I lower myself to the mystery, clinging to the master eagle. As long as he bears most of my weight, I know I'm safe. I place one foot on the atmospheric surface then lower the other. I feel it beneath my feet, as tangible as the rock cave, as real as standing on the ground.

I plant my hands on his body as I slide toward his beak. He turns his head to peer at me, calm in the midst of this impossibility.

"What is this?"

I have asked the wrong question.

"Did you know of this…place?"

He gestures for a nod then flicks his beak outward and downward. He beckons me to look at something. With no way to know how wide this mystical surface is, I lower myself to the stance of a babe. My head feels light—too light—as I position myself to see what he wants me to see.

He must sense my hesitancy. He lifts himself onto his legs and walks past me, abandoning me in my fright and wonder. I lower myself to my belly as though it offers safety. I'm clinging onto something I can't see. I must trust what I feel.

The master eagle walks forward until he stands two lengths of his body from me. He turns to face me and dips his beak downward.

"You wish for me to see something?"

He nods.

I trust him.

I should crawl. It feels like it would be safer with this satchel strapped to my back. I shake my head at the notion. Whether I stand or crawl makes no difference. I'm still on clouds as solid as stone.

I force myself to stand. Sliding one foot in front of the other, I trace my path to him. My heart pounds in my ears. I feel dizzy and weak, and sweaty and jittery. Logic begs for gravity to send me plummeting to the ground.

When I reach him, I throw my arms around his neck. He takes a step forward. One of his legs hangs free and clear of whatever dream this is.

"This is the edge?"

He nods.

I lower myself to sit, still clinging on whatever bits of him I can grab without tugging his feathers. A sensation of panicked dizziness overwhelms me. As I retreat a few paces on my hands and feet, the satchel scrapes the eerie surface beneath me.

My hands are slick with sweat, and I slip. Only my stomach plummets to the earth. My body remains in the clouds. *On* the clouds.

He stares at me, ruffling a wing and dipping his beak. I

don't want to move, but he wants me to, so I do.

As I crawl toward him, he shifts his dangling leg backward, so only his toes hang free. He's showing me precisely where the edge is located.

I place one hand on his leg for support and inch the other forward until my fingers are in line with his foot. I shift it further until my fingertips feel nothing. They feel what they should.

I crouch so my chin touches the illusion. I force my torso to shift so I can see beyond the edge of this invisible surface in the sky.

The rate of my breath quickens. My throat becomes dry. I feel like I'll faint.

What I see is daunting. *Haunting.* Clouds are below me, but they're different. Smoky. As dark as cinders.

My panting deafens me as I watch the dark clouds pass. They're not clouds of rain. Even if they were, it wouldn't explain the dramatic shift in the atmosphere.

I retreat a few paces and look downward. What I see below me is a stark contrast. Below me is a sky of pure white and vibrant blue.

I shift forward again. Never before have I beheld such a dark, smoldering sky.

"What is this?"

He doesn't answer, and I don't know the right question to ask.

He presents his back to me and flaps his wings. He wishes for me to mount. Relief overwhelms me. This nightmare must end. It's time to go east and forget whatever this is.

I climb onto his back and wrap my arms around him. I expect him to fly eastward, but he turns toward the sky of soot.

He carries me beyond the edge of the invisible surface. My throat tightens too much for me either to scream or beg him to change course. He soars outward then dips his beak, diving into the murk.

This air is thick and dank. My lungs declare it poisonous as I choke and wheeze from the foreignness of it. I plant my face into his feathers.

The further he dives, the more my eyes sting. He dives even lower until the poisonous sky reveals the ground below us. There are structures which look as rotten as the air smells. He levels his path. All I see before me is destruction and decay. These are words I know but have never experienced.

The master eagle soars over a horror of desolation. I have seen something similar…at Institute. At Primary, we watched transmissions of a world like this, a world from the distant past.

What I see and smell is a world we were told we healed. It's a world we were told no longer exists.

Yet, it does.

It's a world of death, it lies beyond an invisible surface in the sky, and the master eagle has revealed it to me.

To be continued...
OuterSphere
(The RAYNE Trilogy #2)

Glossary of Latin Words &
The Standard Noun Forms

Ascensus: (n) ascent, ascending, climb

Aeris: (n) air

   (The Standard – s. aerisma, pl. aerismae)

Aqua: (n) water + mare: (n) sea

   (The Standard – s. aquamarist, pl. aquamarists)

Culina: (n) kitchen

Dies: (n) day; day of

Domus: (n) home; household

Emovere: (v) to move through or out

   (The Standard – s. emovis, pl. emoves)

Familia, familiae: (n) family, families

Filia: (n) daughter

Floresco: (v) to flourish, flower, blossom, thrive

   (The Standard – s. floresca pl. florescae)

Frater: (n) brother

Ignis: (n) fire

   (The Standard – s. ignitior, pl. ignitiors)

Magnes: (adj) magnetic

   (The Standard – s. magnos, pl. magnoves)

Mater: (n) mother

Medicus: (n) doctor

   (The Standard – s. medicum, pl. medica)

Mirificus: (n) marvelous, wonderful, amazing

Nepos: (n) grandson

Nomen: (n) name | completum: (n) complete

Paren, parentes: (n) parent, parents

Pater: (n) father

Per viam: by the way

Provideo: (v) to provide

    (The Standard – s. providior, pl. providiors)

Respectu: with respect

Salvē: (inj) hello, hail, welcome

Sciens: (adj) skilled, expert

Susurrator: (n) whisperer

Terra: (n) earth + costos: (n) keeper; guardian

Villa: (n) house

<u>The RAYNE Trilogy:</u>

<u>Other Books by This Author</u>